A Story Every Day of AUTUMN

Edited by John Howes and Fran Neatherway

First Printing, 2023

ISBN: 9798852873545
Imprint: Independently published

For more information about The Cafe Writers of Rugby,
visit their website, www.rugbycafewriters.com

Introduction

The Comfort Of Autumn

Welcome to the second of our seasonal anthologies. If you are new to the Cafe Writers of Rugby, allow me to introduce us. We were formed as a group about five years ago. Most of us live in the Midlands town of Rugby in the United Kingdom. We come from all walks of life, with different backgrounds and interests - but we have one thing in common: we love writing. So we get together in a cafe once a fortnight and share our latest work. We often have a Writing Challenge; this might be a theme such as 'Hope' or the name of a character or a particular genre such as romance or horror. We try to push ourselves out of our comfort zones.

We decided to publish four seasonal anthologies of stories. The first one was *A Story For Every Day Of Summer*, which you may have already read. (If not, why not?) This is our second offering. It features a story for every day of Autumn and covers September, October and November. You will find stories on themes such as Hallowe'en and Bonfire Night, as well as those with a more general autumnal feel. Most are fiction, but some are memoir and some are diary entries. Some will make you laugh, whilst others might make you a little sad. We hope you enjoy the selection and that there is something for everyone here.

And if you enjoy this book, look out for the next one, not unsurprisingly called *A Story For Every Day Of Winter* which will cover December, January and February.

John Howes
www.rugbycafewriters.com

September

October

November

September

September 1

Once In A Lifetime

My heart was pounding as I hesitated. I'd thought about nothing but this moment for months. Scrap that, for years. And now it was finally happening. I was just one step away.

I wasn't hesitant because of nerves (although, believe me, I was trembling with fear). I was hesitant because the second I moved my foot and it touched that surface, the anticipation was all over with. The moment was real.

Taking a deep breath, I edged my left foot off the final step of the ladder and it made contact with the fine, dusty ground.

Exhilaration exploded through me.

As soon as my right foot was firmly on the barely touched surface, I turned around. I couldn't manage quick movements because of the atmosphere, my suit, and the intense sensations gripping every inch of me, but, as I shuffled around one hundred and eight degrees, the amazement hit me.

It was spectacular. Straight away, Earth caught my attention. It seemed so enormous, so humbling, despite the incredible distance.

My eyes explored more, eagerly scanning the empty, lifeless surroundings that I could only be in awe of.

I decided to take my first step forward, over the pebbles and rocks. The weightlessness on the ship had been liberating, and hugely enjoyable, and this far-reduced gravity was just as extraordinary. It was like a bouncy slow-motion, forcing you to take your time and absorb this wonder, whilst providing a terrific sensation of freedom.

I continued forward to begin my work as the notion of this once-in-a-lifetime journey sank in. I was on the Moon. My life could never be the same again. I was doing something so few people will ever experience. I felt lucky, proud and astounded, suddenly realising just how precious life was.

Lindsay Woodward

September 2

Brushes With Fame

A few weeks ago, I was travelling on the train from Exeter to Tiverton when a tall man walked up the corridor towards me and briefly smiled before stepping onto the platform.

He looked vaguely familiar, but it wasn't until about half an hour later that I realised I'd had a brief, though significant, brush with stardom. The man who had smiled at me was none other than former Radio One DJ and *Top of the Pops* presenter Simon Bates, famous – and some might say infamous – for his romantic heart-tugging *Our Tune* spot which ran for many years on his national morning show.

Bates, now a local radio presenter with BBC Devon, was on his way home, a fact he courteously confirmed when responding to a tweet I sent him.

Now Bates may not be an A-list celebrity any more, but it got me thinking how close each of us comes to stardom, and how many times we criss-cross famous people in our lives. They move in our worlds sometimes and we move in theirs. Only last week, my nephew turned to a man he thought was his uncle in Fortnum and Mason, only to find it was Stephen Fry on a shopping spree.

Nor is this uncommon. Shaun Keveney's excellent and much-missed Radio Six breakfast show had a daily slot in which listeners told of meeting celebrities; my favourite was a man who serviced Monty Don's lawnmower.

So, having reached the grand old age of 50, I started thinking how many stars I had encountered. In a way, I had cheated by spending 20 years as a local newspaper hack. If anyone well-known was coming to town, I was usually dispatched to interview them.

Hence, a conversation with John Cleese about his new book was just a normal day at the office. I also confronted Jeffrey Archer at a Conservative garden party, and interviewed Nigel Lawson while he was still Chancellor of the Exchequer. Two of my interviewees arrived by helicopter – Noel Edmonds, then at the height of his television fame, dropped in to help us with a newspaper appeal; and the late Marquess of Bristol alighted on the lawn of Ickworth House, Bury St Edmunds. Then Princess Diana drove past me as I stood outside the Marriage Guidance Council's headquarters in Rugby - but she never even noticed I was there.

However, these cannot count as genuine claims to fame because they were part of my job. I need to dig deeper...

I know that, whilst on holiday in North Wales, the man running our hotel was the uncle of actress Nerys Hughes, best-known for her part in *The Liver Birds*. But that is fame once-removed. I had sat next to Peter Purves from *Blue Peter* at a charity quiz, but then he lived in the same town as me, so maybe that is not a genuine encounter.

Whilst visiting Scarborough, I got the autograph of Tony Peers, a local impresario who got plenty of airtime in the seventies as one of *The Comedians*, an ITV hit-show which gave a platform to the likes of Bernard Manning, Ken Goodwin and Jim Bowen. But was he still famous? Not many were impressed by my story.

On another family holiday, we stopped at a pub and saw Douglas Rae - presenter of classic 1970s children's programme, *Magpie* - leaning against a wall. Pretty impressive? Not really.

And then I was standing in a bookshop in Leamington Spa and noticed the man next to me was the Labour politician George Robertson. He went on to become Secretary General of Nato. Is that good enough for a celebrity encounter?

I was beginning to think I should give up. I could never compete with my wife's stories. At a party, she was once kissed by Richard O'Sullivan. Yes, *the* Richard O'Sullivan, star of *Man About the House* and *Robin's Nest*, and who featured in a television advertisement for gas fires, which ended with the line: "But does it make toast? Yes, it makes great toast." Not only that, my wife had once come across newsreader Peter Sissons buying a pair of shoes, and had shared a coffee with jazz legend, and total gentleman, Johnny Dankworth.

Even my mother was once a bridesmaid at the wedding of Sixties pop legend Billy J Kramer.

Oh, who could it be? What was my life-changing experience? And then it came to me.

I was on an underground train after seeing a West End show. Not next to me, but next-but-one to me, a distinguished looking tall gentleman sat primly minding his own business and holding a bag from an obviously classy clothing store. Maybe a silk tie or handkerchief was contained therein. Who was he? No-one else seemed to be bothered; they were all staring at their mobile phones and plugged into their music. But it was Bill Nighy, star of *Love Actually*, *Pride* and *Harry Potter*, and one of my favourite actors. Just inches from me. But did I say anything? Did I lean over and tell him his role in *The Bookshop* with Emily Mortimer contained one of my favourite ever scenes on film? Did I ask for a selfie? No. I did nothing. I respected his privacy and, when he got off at Camden, I looked around the carriage to see if anyone shared my sense of awe.

Nobody even looked up. They just carried on swiping the screens of their phones, totally unaware that one of Britain's finest actors had just departed the scene.

I'm not sure this counts as a celebrity encounter because Mr Nighy never knew I was there - but I don't mind. It was a brush with fame which I will never forget.

John Howes

September 3

As The Bombs Fell

I had not been asleep long when I was woken by the roar of aeroplane engines. I leapt out of bed, pulled back the blackout curtains and looked up at the sky. A formation of Messerschmitts came into view. My heart began to pound. I ran out of my bedroom and along the landing, pushing open the bedroom doors of my young brother and sister and shouting, "Get up!"

Mum's bedroom was at the end of the landing. I burst in. "Mum, take the children to the Anderson shelter."

While my mother put on her dressing gown, my brother and sister stumbled out of their rooms half-asleep. "Go downstairs, put on your shoes, hats and coats, and go to the shelter," I ordered.

"What about Lily?" Mum asked.

"I'll bring her."

I work long hours in the armaments factory, and Mum thought it best for me if my daughter, Lily, slept in her room during the week.

Mum left her bedroom as quickly as her legs would carry her and followed my brother and sister downstairs.

Lily started to cry. I lifted her from her cot and cradled her. I heard the high-pitch wail of the air raid siren followed by the low drone of heavy aircraft before the deafening sound of exploding bombs. The house shook, the windows blew in, and the bedroom door slammed.

With my crying child in my arms, I lay on the floor and wriggled until we were under the bed. Choking from brick dust and smoke, and shivering as much from fear as from the cold night air, I held my baby close. I sang to her as wave after wave of German incendiary bombs tore through the city. I felt a sudden excruciating pain in my back. It soon passed. Lily stopped crying, and I closed my eyes.

Madalyn Morgan

September 4

The Mysterious Day

It was a Tuesday in November 2020 in ordinary Covid times and I was wishing my daily exercise would take me away from the pandemic.

As heavy showers were forecast, I donned my short green wellies, long black cagoule, blue boat design scarf, a black and red cap and clutched my large black umbrella tightly in my left hand. Ready for any eventuality, I stowed my mobile, front door key, antibacterial gel, blue woolly gloves, a mask and tissues in my black backpack. I like to be prepared.

I was alone on the old Great Central railway line, no dog walkers, nobody else from its entrance to the far corner, about three quarters of a mile of straight track.

In 1969 Beeching had shut the railway line and many others throughout the country. There were tell-tale signs of the old steam trains having blackened bricks under bridges and sloping banks each side where the line had been dug out of the earth to make it flat and safe for the trains of fifty years ago.

It was another miserable, grey overcast morning; no bird song, no cows mooing, nobody calling their dogs, no usual morning sounds.

There was silence. Suddenly, there was a sudden heavy downpour. I opened my umbrella to protect me.

Without warning, there was a whoosh of wind from the children's park on my left; another gust from the right took me totally by surprise and into outer space.

I was in a train carriage, a single carriage. I couldn't see steam or hear an engine. It didn't make sense; there wasn't a driver. I felt an overwhelming sense of peace, safe, escaping from a scary Covid world.

Where was I going? Should I be frightened? Looking through the windows, I noticed grassy fields, grazing cows and sheep whizzing past.

Was I alone? There was nobody else in the carriage. Was I travelling to heaven? I wasn't nervous or worried.

There was nothing I could do when I stopped suddenly with a jolt. The sky was a Mediterranean turquoise blue, the sun shone brightly. I waited for something, someone, a message.

Without warning I was back walking along the old railway line with dog walkers.

Be careful what you wish for.

Kate A Harris

September 5

That's What Marriage Is About

"Do you still love me?" He was standing in the doorway, watching her get ready.

The question caught her off guard and she froze, lipstick in hand. It was one of those questions that has no good answer, like, "Have you stopped beating your wife?"

"Of course I do, darling," sounded insincere, a reflex response, and "Yes," was so blunt, as if she didn't care.

She said quickly, "That's a strange thing to ask on our anniversary."

"Sometimes it seems as if you're just going through the motions."

She went on the attack. "Is that how you feel?"

"What? No, of course not." He was defensive. "Lately you've become so distant. We don't talk any more, or do things together like we used to."

"We're doing something together now." She put the lipstick down and stood up.

"Only because I organised it. You didn't want a fuss, you said."

"And I still don't. You know I don't like parties. There'll be people all over my house, invading my space, judging me." She knew she was whining but she couldn't stop herself.

"We're going to have dinner and drinks with our family and friends. It'll be fine," he said wearily.

They'd been having this discussion for weeks now. "I'll have to talk to everyone." She sighed. "And you know I don't drink."

"I know," he said. "You don't like the taste."

At the same time, she said, "I don't like the taste."

Their eyes met and they laughed. "See, we are doing something together!" she said.

"Come on, my angel. Be brave." He took her hand and they went downstairs.

The living room was empty. "Where is everyone?" He led her into the dining room. The table was laid with their best china and cutlery; the wine glasses her parents gave them when they married. In the centre was a beautiful bouquet of flowers.

"I thought we'd have dinner by ourselves, like it used to be when we first met. Remember how we used to talk the night away?"

She smiled. "Yes, we did, didn't we? When did that stop?"

"Children, work, life," he said. "We always said we'd make time for us, but somehow things got in the way."

She remembered how they used to be, when everything was new and exciting. Life was a rut now, a comfortable rut, but still a rut. "You're right," she said. "But we can change." She leant across the table and kissed him.

They ate and talked and laughed, and the time flew away from them.

"What time is everyone arriving?" she said eventually.

"They're not," he said. "Just us." He raised his glass of sparkling water. "To my beautiful wife. Happy silver anniversary."

There were tears in her eyes. She knew he'd wanted a big party and so she had agreed, because that's what marriage is about. But he knew she'd hate it, and he had done this for her.

"Yes," she said. "Yes, I still love you." And she meant it.

Fran Neatherway

September 6

The Art Of Standing Still

The first taxi in the queue inches forward as we walk out of the station foyer. We don't really care that it is an old heap of scrap metal, tatty faux leather, disintegrating carpet, and heaven knows what is under the bonnet, so long as it takes us home to a warm fire and feet up on the sofa, a five-minute trip, five pounds including tip.

So, he turns off the main road to town, takes the short-cut towards the park. Excellent.

Ah, but no, there's a lorry parked right across the road at the first corner, a massive lorry, and there's one little man loading a skip. It must be his first time, and he's learning the ropes, that is: the winches, cables, hooks, chains. He's taking his time, climbing up and down, road to platform and back again.

There's already an extra pound on the clock, ticking the time in twenty-pence lots, and he still hasn't hooked up the skip hidden round the corner. But here it comes, loaded well over the gunwales, dropping plaster-board, cement bags, bits of nondescript metal all over the road. Our nerves are working overtime. My eyes are glued on the clock. There's a build up of vehicles behind us, so we're stuck.

He's back on the road picking up junk, but he can't reach to put it all in the skip so it's back up on the platform, winch, wind, lower skip, climb down, rubbish in, raise skip, and I'm doing the maths, deducting the waiting fare from the total and not liking the result.

He moves to the cab, opens the door, climbs in, we breathe out. But wait, he has to manoeuvre the lorry to turn it down the road the way we are heading. And, yes, we have to pay the full fare.

Wendy Goulstone

September 7

Sushi Lady

Many years ago, I still lived with my folks in a small English town. My father was ever the moderniser, the extender, the updater, and our house desperately needed an extension

During the early stages, my father dug a two-metre deep hole for the main drain which was in the wrong place, meaning he had to dig across, moving a lot of soil fifty centimetres while he was in the pit himself. Finding out about this, my brother and I sympathetically laughed our heads off

Things progressed a little. One rainy evening, I needed to adjust the tarpaulin that served as a temporary roof patch. As the rain lashed onto our work, I balanced precariously on a loose window lintel like a surfer and was almost wiped out - which would have made this story quite difficult to write. The Singhs from number 11 made a thumbs-up sign.

Our left-hand next-door neighbours were amused by our antics on several occasions. One time, the work involved scaffolding on our more mysterious right-hand neighbours' side; the Japanese side! To avoid an international incident, we had to discuss scaffolding on their property. This unusual circumstance was caused by the local manufacturing company we can call Wakizashi Ltd using that property as a boarding house for male executives with one English female as some kind of liaison? Matron? Euro Geisha? I don't really know exactly her role and that is the whole point of the story.

I remember meeting in the back garden with at least four executives, Lady Sushi looking something between a blonde Chrissie Hynde and Dot Cotton.

My father explained how several strong scaffolding poles would be required on their property to support the whole of our building structure including strong wooden footings thirty centimetres across.

"I will explain this to Mr Tanaka," said the English woman, referring to the dignified chief executive.

I imagine my father shared my anticipation of looking forward to hearing the English lady's fluent Japanese explanation: "Polos holdo up rufo bildo double quick quick..."

Neither before nor after that have I ever seen my father stifle a large hearty laugh. I turned away, biting my lower lip, eyes watering. I realised that Mr Tanaka was not quite on the same page, either confused by the proposition itself or by Dot's pigeon English or whatever that was. I turned to another executive in a tie and white shirt.

"Did you understand that?" I asked the junior Japanese executive in simple English.

"Completely simple. I'm sure it will be fine but I will run it by my boss later to make sure he gets the fine points".

In other words his English was perfect, better than many native speakers. We finished the extension in a few more weeks.

Now and then, when I consider my father's life, I often think of this encounter to help me remember his happy side, the sense of humour now long gone.

Chris Wright

September 8

The Parrot

We have always tried to help neighbours and friends when they go on holiday, feeding their cats, or minding their budgie, but one year, a while ago, it became a little out of hand.

First of all, the harbour master asked if we would look after his parrot. This was going to be interesting as this was a talking parrot; no problem as he was in a cage, and was never let out. At the time, I was almost due to have my second daughter, and my father was coming to stay for six months. About two weeks later, the accountant came to visit and asked if we would mind having his dog while he was on leave (on holiday for two months). Of course we wouldn't. To cap the requests, the assistant manager asked if we would feed his cat. He had to make an unexpected trip.

We entered a very entertaining period of our lives.

First of all, the parrot turned out to be an incredible mimic. He could imitate a Land Rover's gear change, but not only when the Land Rover was there. So on occasion I would think John had come home mid-morning or indeed anytime during the day. I was making bread rolls one day when my neighbour came running out of breath because the bird's cage was outside and she thought I had gone into labour. He had mimicked me calling her name.

After my daughter was born, he could copy her cry and the delivery boys' call as they delivered bread or meat, He only had to hear a sound to imitate it. I could go on at some length about his exploits. Shall we say that on the return of the harbour master, he (the parrot) had to be rehoused as their daughter had two-year-old tantrums and they became a little tiresome.

There was an electrician who had been on the island many years with his wife. They lived next to the harbour master and had never had problems until one day the wife was having a shower when there was a wolf whistle quite clear and close. She thought she had been quite private in her bathroom so was quite annoyed. The sorry story ended with the police being involved, accusations in all directions until the bird let it be known who had whistled. The combination of the tantrums and the wolf whistle meant that the rehousing became essential. The local priest was returning to the Gilbert Islands, and the men returning loved the bird, so he took it with him and we heard no more of our friend.

He left us with so many memories and stories to tell. I still miss him and wish we could have kept him. In the meantime, we had the dog (a boxer with a lovely nature) and the cat, who did, on occasion, chase each other through the house. It may be remembered that the dog was a full grown boxer so life did have its moments.

Pam Barton

September 9

Albert And Mary

Albert had to be alone with his feelings. After spending the previous evening with Mary, he didn't know what to think. She had said that she loved him, and he - he had blurted out that he loved her too. He had meant it at the time, but where was it all going?

He'd known Mary for about a year and a half, and knew she was kind, confident and committed: she wouldn't have said she loved him unless she meant it.

Could they make something of it? They were both free to marry.

And it could all depend on The Letter. The Letter which would probably arrive tomorrow. What would Albert do in the meantime?

Albert heard the sound of the letter-box. He went and saw a letter on the mat. Perhaps The Letter had arrived a day earlier than he was expecting.

He opened the letter and read it:

"Dear Mr. Slater, we are pleased to offer you a place to study at the Venerable English College in Rome. If you want to accept, please reply before the fourteenth of July."

Albert sank into his armchair and said to himself, "What do I do now?"

(The English College in Rome is a Roman Catholic seminary).

Jim Hicks

September 10

Ireland: A Personal Perspective

'The Land of Saints and Scholars.' So says the well-known phrase describing the Irish Republic. A less-kind observer, in search of a similarly alliterative moniker, might say 'The Land of Poets and Pouring Rain.' Both are true up to a point, but there's more to this 32,500 square mile island of less than five million inhabitants than either phrase sums up.

I know Ireland because my wife, Bernadette, comes from Cork, the second city. I first visited in 2000, when I had known Bernadette for about four months. It was the traditional 'meet the family' trip, which was fun and enlightening.

Deep down, I didn't want to go. I wanted to meet my future wife's family all right, but the thought of using precious holiday to go anywhere other than my beloved France didn't excite me. What I found, though, is that Ireland, especially from Cork westwards, does resemble the parts of France I love the most: Brittany, down into the Vendee and the islands off the coast there. The landscape, the buildings, the pace of life, the flora and yes, even the weather. The wonderful local cooking too, based as it is on the abundance of seafood in the area, is not that far removed.

I set about my familiarisation with Ireland by staying true to my own rule: forget the tourist traps and speak with the locals in small cafés, local shops and restaurants, to get a true impression of the country. This is easy to do anywhere in Ireland as most people are up for a chat, especially if there's a coffee or a beer to be chatted over!

Ireland now occupies a place in my heart as somewhere I feel drawn to visit frequently. Go and discover it for yourself though. Don't take my word for it.

Simon Parker

September 11

Colour Prejudice

The Gingers of our acquaintance are easily noticed. It is their fate to become instant celebrities. Their colour, sometimes disliked, is never forgotten. It becomes their badge of identity.

I didn't know his name but knew he must live somewhere in the neighbourhood. I noticed him straightaway, strolling rather jauntily past at various times of the day.

There goes Ginger, I would say to myself. New round here. Wonder where he lives? How old I wonder? Just short of middle-aged – no, younger. Fit. Nicely-built. Can't quite see but it looks as if he goes to that house right at the end, where the street curves. Makes it difficult to tell. The one with the dog, and the female kitten that's friendly with mine.

Mine was a rescue. Had to pay, but she came wormed, deflea-ed and spayed. Friendly with me but very wary of strangers. Not a bad thing.

She'll sit at the end of the drive, guarding her limits, or just being nosey like me – who knows what goes on in a cat's mind?

And then one day Ginger stopped outside. It was friendship at first sight. My cat loved the fuss he made of her and when he strolled on, she followed! It was summer. I knew all cats go into summer mode, but then she began only coming home for meals, or the occasional brief snooze. Otherwise AWOL. I was feeding a non-pet. At least no one else was feeding her. But I no longer had a cat.

The woman at the end house told me she'd seen her with Ginger several streets away – "It's a real romance!" she simpered, but wasn't sure where he lived. As fellow cat-owners we indulged in Moggy Talk when we occasionally met. The kitten she'd taken to the vet's to be spayed, she told me, had turned out to be pregnant. She hadn't been quick enough; Ginger had beaten her to it. Sometimes at night, I heard him calling and then mine thundering down the stairs and the cat flap go. I can't imagine what the attraction was, for she was neutered but they were, to quote another Ginger (Duchess Fergie) the 'bestest of friends'.

My neighbour's cat had four kittens, not one of them ginger.

Chris Rowe

September 12

Late Holiday

Autumn was starting late. The trees were still in full leaf, and very green. And the sun was very bright and very warm. Unfortunately this encouraged retired couples to take extra, late, holidays, and so the usually empty wide stretch of sand along the bay was not as clear as it normally was in this week. The week she always took her one and only holiday each year, specifically because there would be no-one else around.

Until this year it had usually been just the two of them, once the local dog-walkers had buggered off, and they'd had the whole beach to themselves. And not just when it rained. She sighed, remembering. They would run in and out of the sea, play silly beach games, walk along the strand line all the way up to the cliffs, or the other way to the estuary, and not see another person. Bliss.

She stood knee deep in the sea. The waves were fiddling-small. She wanted breakers so that she could bodysurf back to dry sand, with the sea bubbling and roaring in her ears, while abandoned shells bowled past, in the cloudy water below her.

But it wasn't going to be the same this year, anyway, because she would have been surfing on her own, not racing Graham, wrestling with his boogie-board, trying to keep his face out of the water. Always good for a laugh. No laughing this year. She launched herself into the sea, but not to try and ride in, just to swim parallel to the shore. Safer, as she was on her own.

The day felt flat and joyless. Empty. The beach, though, was scattered with huge golfing umbrellas and gaudy windbreaks. Far too many groups of grandparents, young mother and toddler, or mature couples reading their newspapers and unpacking their picnic boxes. Too many loud voices ringing out, and too much complaining, she noted, about the sand on the wind, the lack of a tea-bar, and the antisocial fencing round the sand dunes.

"Well go away then," she muttered to herself. "There's a nice resort a few miles down the coast that will answer all your needs and suit you well. Go there, and leave me in peace."

Her holiday felt spoilt in more ways than one. Not just the burning sun instead of the soft rain, not just the intrusion of all these other people, moaning, and not just because of the limitations this year. No, it was mainly because of Graham, which meant no racing down the beach into the waves, no mock wrestling over who had won the sandcastle challenge, and no bringing home large pieces of interesting driftwood. And she was tired. There'd been no sharing of the driving this year.

She shaded her eyes and looked up the beach, searching along the line of the sand dunes. And there he was, looking just as frustrated as she felt. Maybe they really should have cancelled their holiday after all, but Graham had insisted. He knew how much this week, this place, meant to her, and he couldn't let her miss out. He waved. Did he think she couldn't find him? She smiled and waved back. Then hurried to take hold of his arm, and one of his crutches, as he struggled to his feet, and dusted sand off his plaster cast.

Next year, she thought, we'll leave cleaning out the gutters until after our holiday.

EE Blythe

September 13

Cutting Edge Science

"Is it safe?"

"Darling, this is the cutting edge of science."

My wife was sounding doubtful. I explained as carefully as I could and then she got it.

"You're going to be placed in a body scanner. They will completely reconfigure your DNA and you will emerge changed. Completely changed into a different species. A fish," she said.

"Exactly."

"Why a fish?"

"It's more of a biological challenge, and besides, you know how much I like the water."

"And then, after thirty days, they will repeat the process and you will re-emerge as you were."

"Exactly."

"Just think of the accolades. And think of the book deal: *My Life as a Fish!*"

It all went very smoothly. A moment of darkness as I went into the body scanner, a sudden flash, a sudden headache and a desire to wipe my brow.

Except I couldn't. I no longer had arms but gills. Before me swayed fronds of seagrass, I inhaled and exhaled oxygen perfectly, and oh, that feeling of lightness in the water, the sheer delight of just existing without exam papers to mark, students to scold. There was no doubt about it; life as an aquatic species was pure bliss.

My wife posted notes of reassurance on the side of the tank and I'd nod my head in recognition. The university was delighted.

The children were impressed. They had a celebrity father. They transferred me to a smaller tank inside my own home.

I just wished the cleaning lady hadn't left the back door open the way she did. The big tabby cat from next door sneaked in, and was sitting inches away from the lip of the tank. Staring at me. And not in a nice way.

Simon Grenville

September 14

Unclean

Mary was sitting alone in the small room, waiting. There was a window up high, letting shafts of sunlight flash across the ceiling. She sat on the plastic chair, leaning on her elbows at the little table, waiting.

She looked at her hands; her fingers were red and sore. Her nails were bitten down, and the skin around them had been bleeding. She was picking at the skin. Sad little hands, she thought, but clean.

She took a deep breath and sucked in the smell of the soap from her skin. Mmmm, it was lovely, lovely to be clean.

As a child Mary was never really clean. She had that berry brown weathered look from the hours spent outside in all weathers. Her hair hung in rats' tails, clinging to her face; it was always greasy, always smelly.

Her smell was a mixture of cigarette smoke, mixed with the odours of natural body functions which stuck to her skin and never washed out of her clothes. The clothes were always damp, which added to the mix, which, if it could be bottled, would be called Poverty or Neglect.

There were five children in Mary's family, two older girls and two younger brothers. On bath nights, which were few and far between, Mary got the cold scummy water left over from her sisters. The boys got fresh water and often bathed together.

She held the neck of her clean grey sweat shirt open, and she bent her head to inhale the sweet flowery clean. She closed her eyes and waited.

She remembered the day that she had done it, that terrible, wicked thing that only a naughty, dirty girl would do. A different Mary, a long time ago Mary. A frightened, confused, smelly Mary, who had no one she could tell her secret to, no one to help her, a desperate, desolate Mary.

Now a clean and sweet-smelling, sad Mary, still alone, desperate, and desolate and waiting.

Now the world knew her secret, there was no hiding place and she was afraid of what would happen next. She was waiting.

Linda Slate

September 15

Pharaoh's Bath

Eleanor in her Sunday best hugged the back of the crowd and watched Pharaoh taking his bath in an aluminium tub in the garden. His new skin was gold in the African sun.

It was warm that day two months ago when she opened the closet under the sink at her home in Bulawayo and saw the six-foot Egyptian cobra. She slammed and locked the cupboard door, hoping it couldn't slip through solid wood.

Vultures flapped their wings in her stomach and she knew the fear that evil brings. In Africa, snakes only come into your life because a witch sends them to kill you. Who could hate her family that much? They were honest church-going people.

When her husband, Tafara, came home, they decided to leave the snake where it was. It would soon disappear and go back to the person who had sent it.

Sunday, six weeks later, Tafara thought it was safe to unlock the cupboard and the snake was still there. Just a thin spine with loose, dead skin hanging off it. Motionless, with glazed, blind eyes. He called the police and asked what to do.

Within an hour there was a knock at the door. Not the police but someone from animal welfare.

"You realise you could be prosecuted for this?" said the man who introduced himself as Peter. He was a government biologist and in charge of 'urban wildlife'.

"But you can't be cruel to a snake," said Tafara.

"Yes, they can feel pain and thirst, and this snake is almost dead from dehydration."

Peter said he'd give it a series of warm baths, and antibiotics, explaining that reptiles can 'rehydrate' through the skin. "And food when he's stronger."

"Then are you going to kill it?" asked Eleanor.

"No, I'll let it go on a farm where it can keep down the rats," he said.

But his final words chilled her. "Where are you going to keep it?" she asked.

"Next door," said Peter. "We've never met, but I'm your neighbour."

The following day and every day after that, Eleanor peeped through the curtains and watched while Peter gave the cobra he'd named Pharaoh a warm bath in the garden.

Maybe he was a witch.

Her three young children weren't so scared. They had learned about snakes at school and asked if they could go and watch Pharaoh being bathed.

"Ask Mr Peter nicely and keep well back," said Eleanor.

Then the youngest, Enock, brought a drawing of the snake home from class.

"Why would you draw a snake?" asked Eleanor.

"The whole class did," said Enock. "Mr Peter came and gave a talk and he brought Pharaoh."

When they had a cold snap for a few days, Peter asked Eleanor if he could borrow a hot water bottle. She took it over and saw Peter had Pharaoh in a large, airy cage in a spare room. He filled the bottle with warm water and the snake curled up on it.

Soon, neighbours came to watch Pharaoh at bath time. He was stronger now, and although Peter always handled the snake with a long grip-stick and never put his hand near its head, it seemed to have become quite tame.

Even their priest, Father Joseph, came to look. He'd always said snakes were evil, but when Pharaoh got a stomach infection from some baby food Peter had pumped into him with a catheter, Father Joseph said a prayer in church for the reptile's recovery.

Now, this Sunday it seemed the whole suburb had come to see Pharaoh take his last bath before being released. He had shed his skin and there was a new coat of golden scales underneath.

Eleanor moved forward. Peter had taken Pharaoh out of the tub and was holding him behind the head with one hand and near the tail with the other.

"Can I touch him?" Eleanor asked. Peter nodded and she reached out and felt his smooth, soft skin.

"I'm sorry," she said quietly. "I didn't understand."

Without Pharaoh, afternoons weren't the same. The local entertainment was gone, but things were busy because Eleanor had got to know everyone in the street. Lived in the same area for years but no one had made the effort.

People who used to kill snakes in their gardens now called Peter to remove them. But Eleanor knew better. After Pharaoh, the house was plagued by rats. Now, as if by magic they had vanished and she suspected someone new was living in the garden and raiding the kitchen.

He - or she - was a welcome guest.

Geoff Hill

September 16

Ambrose's Discovery

Ambrose was an ambitious young man who was prepared to travel all over the country to find better paid work and promote his career. He was married to Cecile who happily followed him around the country. They had been married for five years now.

This latest move was to Clithero in Lancashire. Cecile soon found herself a new job, and they found a new house and set about making new friends and acquaintances. Once they were settled, Ambrose decided it was probably time to start a family. The only fly in the ointment was Cecile's monthly night out. It usually coincided with a full moon. She was certainly entitled to her night out, and she never begrudged him his nights out at the pub with the boys. But, he decided, he ought to know what her night entailed.

So he followed her one night using his bicycle and keeping well back, and silent, up Pedle Hill they went. Ambrose lay behind a tussock of grass to watch proceedings. There was an enormous bonfire burning and many women of all shapes and sizes and ages, all singing and dancing and naked. Without a sound, he turned and walked away!

Ruth Hughes

September 17

An Alternative Ending

Now it so happened that the cart passed over some very rough ground and the coffin, which was being carried upon the cart, was severely shaken, causing a piece of poisoned apple to be dislodged from the mouth of the beautiful maiden within. She immediately drew a sharp breath, opened her eyes, threw off the glass lid above her and sat up.

"Oh dear! where am I?" cried she.

The king's son answered, full of joy, "You are near me," and, relating all that had happened, he said, "I would rather have you than anything in the world. I was captivated by your beauty; so wondrous, so serene. Having laid eyes upon you, I could not avert my gaze. I begged with all the passion that your perfect form had stirred within my heart that I be allowed to transport you to my castle, where I could henceforth contemplate your exquisiteness for as long as I live."

He paused and sighed in disbelief, reaching out towards her. She took his hands, was raised to her feet and stepped, lightly and gracefully, from the coffin.

"Such joy and delight, my Princess. By what marvellous miracle have you become mine in both flesh and spirit? I will take you for my bride and you shall live a life worthy of your grace, elegance and charm."

"No!" she exclaimed in distress, "That cannot be. Where are they, my friends, those I live with and serve?"

"Those pitiful dwarves? Why they are probably moping still in their meagre cottage at the foot of the mountain," responded the King's son.

"But I must be with them. Life, indeed, has been restored to me and I must return home."

"You do not understand," said the King's son. "I have liberated you and thus accomplished your miraculous restoration to life. I will bestow upon you riches beyond your imagining; luxury that surpasses all your experience; fame and adoration that befits your utter beauty."

"And there is much that you do not understand, it seems. I know a great deal about the world you wish to flaunt me in and I tell you this: I cannot imagine even the smallest amount of riches that will not taint and corrupt its recipients; my experience of the sort of luxuries you are able to offer, shows they lead only to emptiness and discontent; craving the shallow adoration and flattery of others, breeds nothing but jealousy and hatred. It would have been so much better for you had I remained a perfectly preserved corpse under your ownership and control, available to serve your vanity alone. I know where true riches, luxuries and fulfilment lie."

She cast a brief, pitying glance at the King's son, leapt from the cart and strode purposefully into the woods.

Steve Redshaw

September 18

In A Spin

An extract from my diary

Horrible o'clock in the morning. Having had a rather unproductive week, the terrible "Must Do Better" part of me had set the alarm on Friday night for 7am on Saturday so I could (it gets worse) GO TO THE GYM and (even worse) GO TO A SPIN CLASS.

Trying not to weep, I forced myself out of bed and put on my gym clothes, all the while trying to resist slamming doors resentfully and spraying deodorant too loudly in case of waking the other, luckier members of my family still sleeping upstairs.

Went downstairs and ate a banana. Previous experience of Spin had taught me that not enough food would make me want to throw up mid-class. However I resisted toast as previous experience had also taught me that too much food would also make me want to throw up mid-class.

The cat greeted me with a mixture of delight and surprise and since no-one else had so far, I gave in and fed him. He duly ate and trotted outside to start his morning shift – he works security on the missing fence area in our back garden. To give him credit he has never complained about the lack of decent pay (we don't believe in premium brand cat food in our house) or working conditions but I have frequently seen him sleeping on the job, so fair's fair.

Got to Spin and moaned, yawned and over-fiddled with the bike settings as usual. But then we all do. It's part of the warm-up. To my horror, my normal bike was occupied by an interloper. Sat on a different bike in a different area of the studio and tried not to feel like the worst kind of tourist whose usual sunbed has been usurped.

The music started and it was great. Great enough for me to ignore the sweat trickling down my face, gathering in pools in the bags under my eyes and making my palms stickier than a toddler's.

We sprinted, we climbed, we cycled while standing, we cycled while sitting, we slowed down and sped up. Somehow, 45 minutes passed. Exhilarated, soaked and smug, we disembarked our exercise-steeds and returned home.

The cat greeted me with a mixture of mild disinterest and boredom. I banged the front door shut behind me as loudly as I could, sighed dramatically and kicked off my offensive-smelling trainers. I thumped up the stairs, triumphant.

But still they all slept.

Sally Harper

September 19

Cats

For the first time in their lives, they found themselves the subject of deep scrutiny. It all started out innocuously enough, with a quiet 'miaow' at the open kitchen door, which they correctly translated to mean 'a saucer of milk, please'. The level of engagement gradually escalated to actual entry into the kitchen by the scrutineer, followed by a slow walkabout of the whole ground floor of the house. The visits became more frequent, from once or twice a week to every day, and almost always around the same time. It occurred to them that the s Scrutineer might be working to a plan, but the end game was not at all clear.

The Scrutineer, as you've probably gathered by now, was a member of the local feline community. A tom of slight build and indeterminate age, but certainly no more than three years. He had a sleek black coat with a smudge of white around his nose and four white socks. They mused that maybe he might be called Socks, and the name stuck.

The affair became a topic of discussion at their occasional dinner parties. Advice from their guests varied wildly from 'give him the boot now or you'll have him for life' from the softest animal lover among them, just trying to be sensationalist, to 'make a bed for him in the corner of the kitchen and entice him to stay overnight' from the more level-headed (and less inebriated) members of their small group.

In the end, the decision was made for them. One Saturday morning, Socks greeted them at the foot of their bed with a series of loud 'miaows' and several flicks of his long, shiny tail. A signal to them that they'd passed the test and that he was here to stay!

Simon Parker

September 20

What She Needed To Do

"Do you still love me?" What a strange question. Of course, I did. I picked up my glass of champagne and leaned back in my chair. Although, come to think of it, when was the last time I'd told her? I looked out at the last remnants of the sunset. On this day of looking back, I tried to remember the first time.

It hadn't been when we were courting. No, that's not the right phrase, we're not that old: when we were going out. Young men didn't say that sort of thing to girls. It must have been when I proposed. What a muddle that had been. I wanted to do something romantic, but finding the right moment, getting down on one knee and producing a ring, all at the same time, ended in chaos. Had I told her I loved her? I think I forgot that, but she said yes.

It must have been when we married then. I remembered a long discussion with the vicar about whether she would promise to obey me, or not. What did we decide in the end? Everything else is a blur of flowers and dresses and relatives I never met again. But tell her I loved her? I don't know.

Children came. I know I told my daughter I loved her, I'm not sure about my son. Everyone was happy. I bought her flowers, I might have shed the odd tear, but I don't remember saying those words.

The years passed. I wrote it in every Christmas and birthday card: "with all my love". I didn't need to say it.

Now, here we were. It had been a busy day. So many people: friends; relatives, some of whom I needed to be reminded of who they were; children and grandchildren and various other connections. All gone home now, leaving just the two of us.

I looked out over the now dark garden. It had looked perfect for the celebration, and the weather had stayed fine. We had been lucky. I had worked hard and we had a decent house, all paid for now. I had done it all for her. Didn't that show how much I loved her?

I turned and looked at her. She was tired, I could tell, with a faint frown that told me that she was thinking of what she needed to do tomorrow. She looked old, but beneath it all she was still the same girl that I had fallen in love with all those years ago. I was ashamed that I couldn't remember ever telling her that I loved her. Surely, she knew? If I hadn't said it before, what was the point of saying it now? I took another sip of champagne and the bubbles filled my head.

"Of course, I still love you. I always have and I always will. Happy anniversary." I tilted my glass and we drank a toast. She didn't say anything but the frown had turned to a smile.

Christine Hancock

September 21

I Remember When

There was a bright flash, and a loud bang. The house they were in was hit. Three of them died, including Grandad. The remaining five, two adults and three children, were injured, but not seriously.

They set off in the morning for the border.

'The children look bewildered.'

'I think we all look bewildered.'

It may have been too early for the shock to register. How does that work? It seems some people are very upset immediately and others are stunned for days. 'Bewildered' might be another way of saying 'stunned'.

The weather was cold, and sometimes wet. A doctor might have said they were exhausted, and living on adrenaline.

Flight.

Flight can be slow moving. They couldn't all run the 200 miles to the border. The days went by. A reporter tried to interview them.

Nikita said he had nothing to say. Was he Russian?

'I am a human being, just about.'

After three weeks they arrived at the border. Remarkably, two women, neighbours in their home town, offered to take them all in. The journey to their homes was easier. They had cars. The five of them were shown to their beds, and offered a cooked meal in an hour. All together, in one of the homes.

They lay on their beds, but perhaps it would be an exaggeration to say they rested. Maybe still adrenaline, even after three weeks.

As they were eating, Boyko said, 'Just before we were hit, Grandad said, "I remember when…" He used to say that a lot.'

Sofiy said, 'Grandad Mykola left us a lot of treasures.'

Peter Maudsley

September 22

A Room Without A View

There wasn't anything particularly dull about Brian's house, but all the houses in that row were laid out in exactly the same design. The only differences were in the decoration.

I had visited two of the other houses so I thought I knew what to expect.

How wrong I was.

The lounge seemed a bit dark. I couldn't work out why until I looked at the large window at the back. On the other side, instead of a garden there was another room. I was puzzled. I was even more puzzled when I realised the furniture in this other room looked mostly like the furniture in the lounge, but rearranged. Could it even be the same room?

Brian, who had been hanging my wife's coat up in the lobby, came in and saw my confusion. "Oh," he said. "Perhaps I should have told you. Have you heard of slow glass?"

"Yes," I replied. "Light takes eight hours to pass through slow glass. They put some panels up above the street in Lostwithiel to help illuminate it after dark, as an experiment."

"This," said Brian, indicating the window, "is a panel that went wrong. Light takes a year to go through this. I had it cheap from the factory. Eighteen months ago, my daughter was given a year to live. I had this panel put in, and after she died, I had it removed and put in the other way round."

As if on cue, a young girl appeared on the other side of the window, went over to it and stared in (or out), looking bored and depressed. Perhaps it had been raining.

Brian spoke with a catch in his voice. "So now, I can see her as she was when she was alive, a year ago." He continued to look at the girl, as if waiting for her to go away.

I started to set up the screen and projector. It would be about half an hour before the others arrived. I knew at least one person was going to find it hard to concentrate on my presentation.

Jim Hicks, drawing on two stories by Bob Shaw.

September 23

Against All The Odds

Against all the odds, fourteen-year-old Vladimir – now in his nineties – drew a windmill. Vladimir gave me the windmill (circa 1943) when I left London in 2010.

Vladimir's school years were the same as any other young person born in Ukraine in the early part of the 20th century, except his family were Christians, which was illegal. Vladimir's grandfather was a priest. He hid his calling, as all clergy did in Ukraine after the Russian Revolution of 1917. Priests were executed, or sent to labour camps, Gulags, to be re-educated.

Vladimir was christened in secret. The priest went to his parents' house disguised as a worker – his bible and robes hidden in a workman's holdall. Around that time was the systematic removal of intellectuals, writers and artists. Moscow sent the KGB to execute anyone with enough intelligence to organise a revolution.

With Fascists on one side and Communists on the other, Vladimir's school programme depended on which political party was in power at the time. Military training, however, was always part of the curriculum. Aged ten, he was taught how to use a hand-grenade, assemble and shoot a rifle, and attach and use a bayonet. And, like all Ukrainian children, he had no choice but to join Communist Youth clubs.

February 1942, in snow three metres high and minus twenty degrees, Vladimir and his mother, along with thousands of other people, were taken by the Germans and put on a cattle train, seventy people to a wagon, with no windows. Only when they arrived at the Gulag in Germany were they allowed out of the wagons.

It was in the Gulag that Vladimir – aged fourteen – attended his first church service. He was taught The Creed by the camp's German Chaplain, who gave him pencils and paper.

And, as long as he was back before curfew, the guards allowed him to go out of the camp to practise his drawing.

Seventy-eight years later, Vladimir's pencil sketch of a windmill hangs in pride of place in my sitting room.

Madalyn Morgan

September 24

Holiday Drama

"Oh to be in England -"

"I'd rather be in Spain," my wife snarled, entering the lounge and flopping on the sofa.

"I know," I said through gritted teeth. "And as soon as filming has finished, we'll go away. Now, if you can just let me practise my lines." I composed myself, ready to start my monologue again. "Oh to be in England -"

"It's been over a year since we last went on holiday," she moaned.

I exhaled sharply. "My work has to come first. I've been in high demand. Isn't that a good thing?"

"What's the use in you earning all that money if we can't go away?"

I sat down next to her. "You live in a mansion, you drive a Bentley, you have designer everything. Is that not enough?"

She folded her arms and turned away from me. I sat still until I felt sure she'd given in, then I retook my pose to once again practise my big, Oscar-worthy speech.

"Oh to be in England -"

"I'm not completely materialistic," she cut in.

I sighed. "I know."

"I actually want to go away so we can spend some time together."

I turned to her, my heart softening.

"Okay, I've got a short break from filming next weekend. How about we go on a city break?"

"A city break?" she hollered, like I'd suggested grave digging.

"Yes."

"I want to be sitting on a beach, not trekking around some stuffy city."

"But we'd be together."

"Yeah, together and bored."

I clenched my fists. She never used to be so whiny. My money really had spoiled her.

"If you want a holiday that badly, why don't you go on your own?"

"Really?" she asked, full of hope.

"No!" I yelled back. "We're going together. You only have to wait until filming has finished. Which is going to take longer if you don't let me practise my lines."

"How can you still not know your lines? Even I know them." She stood up, mocking my inspiring stance. "Oh to be in England -"

"You're not being helpful," I said, pushing her aside. "If it's going to make you happy, why don't you plan a holiday and get something booked in? I should be finished in three months. At least it will give you something to look forward to."

"Do you mean it?" she asked with an innocent optimism. I used to fall for that look, before I realised she was pure venom inside.

"Yes. But I want to go somewhere quiet. Somewhere I won't be recognised. Do you understand?"

"All right. Although you know you're not that famous."

She scuttled off with a smile.

Finally I could get back to my practice.

"Oh to be..."

Where was she booking? The stress of where we'd end up started strangling me. I didn't want to go anywhere with jellyfish. Or sharks.

I re-took my stance. I had to practise.

"Oh to be in -"

Oh that could wait. I needed to book a holiday.

Lindsay Woodward

September 25

The Way Back Home

Life has always taken an unexpected turn, and I have found, that when it does, you must go with it. Like the times I would miss the train when I worked in Lutterworth. Late nights and early mornings didn't go together; still, I did have a bike and after a mad dash to the station I would see the porter looking down the road towards me. The road rose in a hump about 200 yards ahead, thus encouraging me to pedal even faster as he waved to me to hurry.

This was usually just time to make it as the train had to wait in Leicester for fifteen minutes before continuing on to Nottingham, giving me time to reach a slightly later train. The usual action was to shout thank you, throw (almost) my bike into the bike protection area and run downstairs where another porter was standing holding a door open for me. Those were the days!

On the occasions when I was too late to actually catch the train, it led to me having an eight-mile cycle ride to ensure I arrived at work on time. This certainly kept me fit, especially as I was fed cheese-filled crackers for breakfast on arrival.

The return home was much more leisurely as the station was very close to the workplace, which was a foundry where I used to type the accounts. It was a very happy place where I planned my wedding, buying the basic crockery from a local hardware shop. I realised that I couldn't continue there after we were married so I applied for an assistant to a production manager, and the distance to work was four streets. Much easier.

I remember really happy memories of that place. The summer that was so hot and no-one worked after twelve pm. Work started at five am. The heat on the production line was unbearable, and I was pregnant, so the afternoons were very welcome, even though I was not in that area.

Pam Barton

September 26

Life Lesson Number One

As a teenager I travelled to secondary school by train. Unusual nowadays, and not common then. Forty, fifty school kids clambering into the carriages, chucking satchels onto the luggage racks, leaning out of windows to screech to their friends, putting their feet up on the seats opposite. The feel of the coarse moquette on bare legs in the summer, the grubby windows, the stuffy overheated atmosphere in winter, the rattle of the carriages over the points – I've never forgotten it.

Some of the carriages were so ancient they still had separate compartments: opposing bench seats, a door out on each side, no linking corridors. Sensible girls like me always avoided those. To get trapped in one with a few of the coarser boys could be, at best, a very unpleasant half-hour. But to be trapped in one of those with only Andrew for company? Tall, slender Andrew, with clear grey eyes and an overlong fringe? Popular Andrew who rarely had his school tie in a neat knot but got away with it by charming the teachers with his crooked smile? Sadly, there was very little chance of that. He was usually surrounded by a gang of cronies and aspiring girlfriends.

But one day he wasn't. As I got into the carriage I saw him and noticed a vacant seat beside him. He glanced up, almost smiled. I hesitated but then the whistle blew and a blonde fifth-former called Vicky leapt in and pushed past me. I put my hand against the door jamb to steady myself. She yanked the door closed and my fingers were caught and crushed in the hinge. I cried out as the pain ran up the nerves in my wrist, and I clutched my hand. Two fingernails were flattened and blood dripped from another. I could not stop myself sobbing from the shock and the fierce, aching pain.

Everyone leapt up. Vicky gasped, "Oh, Diana, oh, I'm so sorry! Oh gosh – look at your hand!"

A capable-looking woman from two rows along stood up and strode towards us. She took my wounded hand in a firm grasp.

"Hmm," she said. "I don't think you've broken anything."

I looked up at her. Was she serious? By now I was shaking and my head was reeling. I felt like my whole hand was fractured.

"Go and run it under the cold tap in the loos for ten minutes," she said, pushing me firmly towards the toilets. "Go on – don't be a baby. You'll be fine."

The train lurched forwards and I stumbled into the toilet cubicle. As the cold water ran over my fingers and wrist, the pain eased. I felt calmer and less sick from the hurt. After ten or twelve minutes I fished out a hanky and wrapped it round my bruised nails. The bleeding had stopped.

I staggered back towards the compartment. Vicky was sitting next to Andrew but she leapt up.

"Are you all right? Oh, I'm so sorry! It was all my fault – I'm so sorry!" she gushed. "That was such a stupid thing to do."

I didn't know what to say and I still felt very odd. Putting my hand to my forehead I swayed sideways and leant against a seat.

"You look so pale – are you going to faint?" she exclaimed.

"Give her a seat, you idiot," Andrew said.

"Oh, yes, here!" she said. "Here you are!"

I sank gratefully onto the seat next to Andrew.

"Does it hurt?" he said, taking my hand and examining the blue-tinged nails.

I nodded. "A bit..." I whispered.

"You're so brave!" Vicky said. "I'd have screamed or fainted or something!"

Shrugging, I managed to blink back a tear and give Andrew a watery, tremulous smile as he looked at me with concern, while Vicky hovered nervously and apologetically over me.

That was over twenty years ago, but I remembered it as I stood in our pristine kitchen and stroked the glossy surface of my brand-new top-of-the-range phone. It was a present from Andrew. He'd forgotten my birthday again. I smiled. That day on the train I learnt my first and most valuable lesson in life. How to use feelings of guilt and pity to get what I wanted.

Cathy Hemsley

September 27

An Afternoon In Autumn

"Do you still love me?"

Always the same question in those big brown eyes, although there'd never been any doubt on either side since they first met. Across the years she would come and watch as he worked and then lay her head on his lap as he slaked his thirst after a tiring Sunday afternoon in the garden. They'd always repaired to this tree, he with his back against it, would survey his handiwork, she content to be close to him in repose.

Today was different. True they were by the tree, but he was digging, as she looked on.

"You all right there, old girl?"

A slight movement of the head acknowledged the question. She would never be better. He put down the spade and bent to caress her.

"Yes, you look comfortable enough."

It had been a mistake to start so close to the tree he realised. The roots of the ugly old sycamore impeded every thrust of the spade and progress was painfully slow, but that particular spot meant so much to both of them that he had no option. And he'd better hurry; a visitor was due in half an hour and he really needed everything in order by the time the man arrived.

And half an hour wasn't much of a substitute for the eternity that he really wanted; for it to never end, this special time together. For them to share it for ever. All too soon reality broke into his reverie. The new arrival came into the garden without formal invitation,

"Anyone about?"

"By the tree; we're over here?"

The two men were not friends exactly, but knew each other, and shared a mutual respect. As ever, he carried a black bag, battered by many forays more arduous than today's.

"So how are things?"

The newcomer was bending down and it wasn't clear who he was addressing. The brown eyes must have recognised the stranger; they'd met on occasion over the years, but this time they showed no suspicion. This time he was accepted as a friend.

"Much the same, but we managed to get out here. This is our special place."

"That wouldn't have been easy. Those old legs can't have got her far, they were bad enough when I saw her earlier."

"I carried her."

"That would have been heavy going, she must be quite a weight, even now."

"We coped."

As they talked the outsider was busy with the tools of his trade and the other sat down so her head could lie on his lap, and the brown eyes could see into his. Slowly, as they looked lovingly at each other for the last time, the light went out of hers and he closed her lids.

"If you're ok here, I'd better get on."

The black bag was repacked and he nodded towards the result of his handiwork.

"Never easy."

No, not easy he thought as he placed her gently in the grave, covering her first, with earth, and then with a paver.

"That'll keep you safe from the foxes."

David J Boulton

September 28

Making Space

Druid looked proudly at the wonderful tangle of brambles and briars, now dark brown and dried up after Autumn, threaded through with trails of dark green ivy, and the dead stems of tall, native grasses. It had taken very little physical effort, really, to get it to this. Most of the hardship had been dealing with the neighbours, who wanted him to 'tidy' his garden. He'd caught the chap from the garden across the end pouring gallons of weedkiller over the fence, and they'd almost come to blows. In the end Druid had set up movement activated cameras, and with this evidence had taken the neighbour to court over it. And won!

He hadn't spoken to the man since, although he still got on well with the wife, Stella. Could have been a bit too well at times, if she'd had her way. In the summer she'd pop round to collect strawberries, raspberries, lettuce or cherries from his garden, and on any excuse would linger to talk with him, preferably over a long, cool glass of something, taken on the 'terrace' or on the grass.

But today, after six years of trial and tribulation, Druid was satisfied with the cover the tangle was providing for small animals, growing as it was over a rough layer of decaying felled tree trunks, and a brashing line of culled shrubbery he'd scrounged from a mate's garden. From his movement cameras he knew that he had hedgehogs, voles and mice using the cover regularly, and foxes on occasion. He'd seen snakes in the compost heap that had been disturbed by a Muntjac, but was still trying to devise a way of deterring the local cats, without alienating the wildlife.

Druid blew on his cold fingers. Yes, winter was definitely knocking on the door. The recent gales had impaled leaves from a nearby beech tree on the thorns of the briar and bramble, and left a deep drift along the fence line, which he was pleased to see. As he headed back to the house he checked the various bird boxes were secure enough to cope with winter storms, and that the greenhouse was securely closed up. Time to go in for a hot drink. That was when he heard his phone ringing, saw it turning 'do-nuts' on the kitchen table.

"David, where have you been?" His mother sounded peeved.

"Sorry, did you need me to do something? I've been right down at the bottom of the garden. I had to replace a fence panel."

"I was hoping you could come and collect the old tin bath. You said you wanted it, and I could do with it out the way. It's too late now, it's going dark." It wasn't, but his mother was nearly eighty, and she battened down the hatches as soon as it looked gloomy, like many old folk did. She asked him if he'd heard from Heather yet, but he hadn't. That was another fence he had to mend.

Heather was a fair bit younger than him and had suddenly decided, after ten years together, that she wanted to start a family, as she put it. His silence, in response to her announcement, had been taken as a negative. And she'd picked up her car keys and left. A bit of an extreme reaction, Druid felt. She wasn't answering her phone when he tried to call her, and he'd left several voice messages, to no avail. He had no idea where she might have gone, and she'd been gone over a month, now.

He made a coffee and sat, for a long time, looking out through the glass doors at his little kingdom. He wasn't sure a swing and a sandpit would fit in, or enhance the view. And what about the wildlife? He wasn't sure he wanted change. But he was missing Heather. He didn't want to be a father, but he did want to be with her, more than anything, and she wanted to be a mother. He glanced at his watch. He'd try phoning again after 8pm. One child wouldn't be too much of a change, would it? It would just be a case of getting used to the idea.

The phone pinged. A text. He glanced at it. Heather!

'David Griffiths, I love you. I miss you. And we need to talk. I'm coming back tomorrow. And you're going to be a dad. It's up to you if you want to be a Dad.'

Oh. It was that real! That soon! Strangely, he didn't hesitate.

'We'd better get married, then' he typed. And with a last look at the garden, where he could already see a place to put a slide, a swing, and even a paddling pool, he pressed *Send*.

EE Blythe

September 29

Madrigal

Irene was born to sing. She'd sing anything, even Country & Western, but she loved the classical choral works best – Faure's *Requiem*, Brahms' *German Requiem*, *Carmina Burana* – and, alas, the nearest proper choir was too far away. A church choir would've done – she liked the Christmas carols and there were some splendid hymns – but the choir at her local church consisted of men and boys only. She was pretty sure that wasn't allowed anymore, but the vicar was a bit of, well quite a lot of a misogynistic arse-hole, and he always had some ridiculous reason for turning down any woman who applied. Irene was tired of fighting wars that she had no chance of winning.

And so she'd joined the madrigal group. She enjoyed the harmonies and the challenge of singing unaccompanied. They sang well together. She'd always thought that madrigals were quintessentially English, but, to her surprise, they originated in 16th century Italy. Or 12th century Italy, depending on what you read. The internet was a wonderful thing, apart from the glaring inaccuracies and the rampant misogyny.

Madrigals reminded her of long summer days, grassy meadows full of butterflies and wildflowers, warm sunshine and gently flowing rivers, *The Hissing of Summer Lawns* by Joni Mitchell, and Henry VIII, who was supposed to have written *Greensleeves*. Then her thoughts filled with death and divorce, suppurating leg ulcers and syphilis, and yet more misogyny. What a pretty word syphilis was for something so ugly. Irene imagined a lost Shakespearean comedy about twins named Syphilis and Chlamydia, a boy and a girl separated at birth, who were forced by a plot depending entirely on coincidence to dress as each other: *The Two Social Diseases of Verona* or *A Condom of Errors*.

Memories of Italy swam to the surface of her mind. Thirty years ago she had visited Florence. The Ponte Vecchio and the Uffizi Gallery were still fresh in her memory, so many beautiful paintings and buildings to admire. If only she'd been able to stay there longer or time-travel back to the Renaissance and meet Michelangelo, Leonardo, Raphael and Donatello. They gambolled through her thoughts. *Teenage Mutant Ninja Turtles*. Her mind was off again, changing direction without so much as by your leave. It had no consideration.

'And they're green,' she sang, looking round quickly to see if anyone had heard. 'I could murder a pizza.'

'What's that, Mum?' Anna said.

'Nothing, dear.'

Anna, home from San Francisco where she worked for one of those dot.com whatevers that sprang up out of nowhere and made obscene amounts of money out of thin air. Irene had wanted to sing professionally. That really would have been making a living out of thin air. And she'd've been happy and maybe Anna wouldn't have left her and gone across the sea.

Irene loved swimming, the feeling of freedom, being weightless, held up by the water, but not in the sea. The salt water made her throat sore. Swimming pools were better, but sometimes the chlorine was too strong and her eyes watered and the taste lingered in her mouth.

She should've visited Anna while she had the chance, but she hated flying. All those people crammed together in such a small space, breathing each other's air. Anna sent emails full of pictures; easier than writing, wasn't it? The Golden Gate Bridge, the old wooden houses, the steep streets, the trams. What else was San Francisco famous for? Hippies and gays. Had Anna sent photos of people too? Or was it her Facebook page where Anna had posted pictures of friends and colleagues? And her lovers, for all that Irene knew.

Irene remembered taking Anna to the ballet, Coppelia was her favourite, and afterwards she'd demanded ballet lessons, but dancing hadn't held her interest. Neither had singing. A shame, considering she'd named her daughter after Anna in *The King and I*. Had she ever told Anna that? Or was it *Anna of the Five Towns*, Irene's A-level English set book? By Alan Bennett, no, it was by Arnold Bennett. Did it really matter?

The words of the *German Requiem* scrolled across her brain. 'Behold, all flesh is as the grass and all the glories of man are as the flowers of the field.'

'Anna,' she said.

'I'm here, Mum.'

'The grass is withered.' And so am I, Irene thought.

Fran Neatherway

September 30

The September Break

Fire, that's what it was in reality, a great big, huge, humongous ball of fire. And where she stood was nothing more than its cooled ashes. As in a way she was herself and everything around. And everything around that. So powerful, so bright, you couldn't look at it. And yet you needed it for a good holiday. Sylvia savoured its presence, closing her eyes and let the September sun warm her upturned face. She smiled and sighed. The old long anticipated sounds were all there: that distant rhythmic swish of waves, the iconic piercing cry of gulls, and with them, the occasional crunch of pebbles and passing comments of other promenaders, fellow Covid refugees. A few days by the sea, how lucky can you get! Took ages for Sheila's girl to fit us in. The town's best rated B and B. And the weather's fine. We're so lucky. Lovely, gorgeous sun.

She glanced at Ed by her side. 'Happy?'

'Er, yes – happier when I get to that golf course, that game they've fixed for me.'

'I'm happy just - promenading - I suppose that's where it comes from, the promenade, just strolling along it.'

'Sooner be strolling on a golf course – there's some purpose to it, then.'

'Relaxing's nice. Just being here. A change.' She smiled at him. He was wearing his golfing jacket. It'd been a bit of a rush for her to get it back from the cleaner's. Especially as they'd had it re-proofed, too. Ed'd insisted on that. It was his favourite jacket. But there was none of that last-minute rush around she'd always had to do when they went in the caravan. Ed always liked to wait and see what the weather'd be doing, so always a last-minute rush for her. But this time, none of that - and no meals to prepare. No getting up before Ed to do the breakfast. He loved waking up to a bacony smell. 'A beckoning bacony smell,' he'd joke, every time he got up.

She'd expected to catch up on family news, while Ed was out golfing. She'd offered to help, but 'No, we have our system. It's all worked out. You go and be a guest, go on out with Ed.'

In the caravan she'd often be doing an evening meal, especially if Ed had been out fishing all day. Sometimes they'd go out together, for a pub meal or bring back a takeaway, especially if there was sport on the telly. Ed didn't care to watch much else. But now, no need to think about an evening meal, except just turn up and eat it.

And now, here they were, strolling along together. In the sunshine.

'That was a fantastic breakfast they gave us. You can see why they won B and B of the Year. I couldn't manage a lunch, but I'm glad we stopped for a coffee. And this hot bake I got will do me for now.' She got it out of her bag. 'D'y want half?'

'No, not hungry yet.' Ed had done full justice to his breakfast.

'I noticed you enjoyed it. You had more than you usually do.'

'We paid for it.'

'Oh, Ed. They're losing money by having us. Could've had ordinary guests. They've only charged us the basic rate – just the cost of the food. Nothing else. No hot water, no linen, no -'

Ed cut her off. 'All right, don't go on about it. But d'you think we'd have got the room if Covid hadn't reduced their numbers?'

Sylvia reflected that they'd been booked in three months ago, but said nothing.

'I'll get something at the golf place. After. They're bound to have something.'

She closed her eyes again, feeling that warm sun on her lids. Ahh, the smell. Old familiar sea front – nature's seaweedy ozone blended with commercial sweet, almost sickly, enticing candy-floss – and fish'n'chips and overpoweringly that hot bake she held in her hand, that oblong, gravy-filled promise. She smiled and inhaled, and opened eyes and mouth.

Thud. A sudden push down hard upon her shoulder. She'd screamed before she knew it. Mugged – in Yarmouth! It happened so fast. So close, too close, a curved white head, a purposeful eye, bright red dot on yellow beak, closing around her bake. Her bake. She clung onto it, jerking her arm away.

Hot gravy spurted out in an arc, down over Ed's jacket. His new-cleaned (and re-proofed) best favourite golfing jacket. His trousers also took on a lesser but matching pattern of drips and trickles.

The gull flew off, defeated. And still hungry. Sylvia had not let go of her savoury bake. Still clutching it, she managed to get out the baby-wipes - so useful to keep in a handbag - mopped up the few splashes on herself, on Ed's trousers, and tried, less successfully, to obliterate the stains on the jacket. Ed was not amused. The jacket had a zip and could be done up to disguise his paunch. It had style. It had class. In it he felt good, and, ungrammatically, played good, too.

Sylvia was a practical woman, and a hungry one. She ate her bake - it was still warm- careful to avoid the bit seized by that hungry beak. That remnant, for she was also a kind woman, she discreetly dropped not in the bin but some feet away. In the open. Ed didn't see, he was too busy grieving over his jacket. Must've been really hungry, poor thing.

Ed played a poor game later, distracted by an unsettling gravy odour every time he swung his arms. Sylvia, wandering around town, treated herself to another hot bake, consumed it on high alert, decided she couldn't finish it all, not really, broke off a quarter, straightened her arm, opened her fingers and let it drop to the ground.

She saw a book in a window with a picture of a gull on it, and went in and bought it.

Chris Rowe

October

October 1

Sisters' Antics

Fiona stood motionless, petrified. Her jaw dropped, her face a deathly white. Her jet black hair wasn't standing on end; it couldn't even if it wanted to. It was long, straight and flowed down to her waist.

"Help, who's there?" Fiona shouted from the attic room.

"What's that loud noise? Is somebody in the cupboard? Let's hope they're stuck!" said Jess as she walked from the room next door to join Fiona.

"I've no idea what just happened to you, but I'm not afraid. You're the scaredy cat," said Jess. 'Try to be sensible for a change. Let's carry on clearing the attic for Mum. It has to be sorted. We promised. Maybe we can do it together.

"Your mouth is open. You look even more gormless than ever. What shall we do? I didn't know the attic was haunted. I don't believe in ghosts. At least I don't think so...

"The photo albums were piled too high. Maybe they made a noise when they fell. There are photos of us when we were children. One album's on the floor, open at that ridiculous photo of you trying to help make rubbish fairy cakes with Mum. Maybe the noise was something else." Jess nattered on, not stopping to take a breath.

She was pretending to be unconcerned and throwing insults at her older sister. Fiona was staring, ashen-faced and unable to speak.

"Auntie Liz's antique chair is on top of the old drop leaf table. I believe she died in this house, about twenty years ago. Mum is downstairs on her own. Dad's gone to a meeting, some parish council business. Why isn't he around when he's needed? Let's find Mum. It's nearly half past five and should be tea time. I hope it's fish fingers and Angel Delight for pudding. Yummy, they're my childhood favourites! What memories."

"What shall we do with that chair, Jess?" Fiona gulped. She was trying not to show her fear. She was the elder sister and should be brave. At that moment she didn't feel brave.

"I think we should leave it alone and get out of this room. Now, please," barked Jess.

Fiona pulled her woolly red cardigan around her ample chest and fastened every button, up to her slender neck.

"Cold, Jess, what can be happening? It's extremely cold. Let's go downstairs. Find Mum!"

They found Mum sitting quietly at the large oak kitchen table in the middle of the farmhouse kitchen. She wasn't listening to the usual Radio 4, not that day. Her hair was recently permed and dyed a lovely mahogany colour. It suited her. She was slicing runner beans for tea.

"Mum, there's something I must ask you," said Jess, trying not to sound too urgent and arouse any suspicion.

"Yes, Jess. Come and help me. You can cut these sliced beans. Make yourself useful. You too, Fiona. What's the matter? You look like you've seen a ghost? I'll turn the heating back on, it's chilly in here."

"Mum, I need to ask you about Aunt Liz. Was she happy?" continued Jess.

"Why ever are you asking about Aunt Liz? She died years ago, maybe twenty years and it would've been her ninetieth birthday today. Yes, today as it happens. She was very poorly and lived here for the last five years of her life. Unfortunately, she was in terrible pain and she made our lives a misery, especially my life. I was her younger sister and she blamed me for her illness."

"Why?" Jess asked.

"It was a very long time ago. Another age..." She hesitated. "Your Dad and I went to the end of the year university ball together. We had a wonderful evening. Sadly, Aunt Liz had failed her degree and couldn't go. Several years later she told me that she fancied your Dad and that I took him away from her."

"Oh, Mum. Poor Aunt Liz. Was it true?" Jess couldn't believe it.

"Not intentionally, of course, but I met your Dad in a local dance. He was in the same year as Aunt Liz at university and they were good friends. But they'd never been on a date. I didn't know she fancied him and she never plucked up the courage to say anything. In those days young ladies waited for the men to ask them out."

"How boring. If I fancy somebody I'll make the first move. Were you prettier than Aunt Liz? Is that why Dad fancied you more?" asked Fiona.

"Something like that. I never knew Aunt Liz felt so angry until she moved in with us and said dreadful things to me."

At last Fiona and Jess had finished cutting up the beans.

"Dad's been to the allotment this morning and returned with this glut of beans. Thanks for helping, girls," said Mum with a sigh.

"Tell us, Mum, about Aunt Liz. We are interested."

"Why the sudden interest? It's years ago and difficult to talk about."

"No reason, it's just..." Jess tried to think of a reason without worrying her mum. Dad had suffered a heart attack six months before and they didn't want to worry either of their parents. She was thinking about the 'presence' in the attic. They had seen the chair move. If it was meant to hit Fiona or Jess, it missed - this time.

"You've never told us much about our aunt. Why?" Jess continued, attempting to keep her composure.

"Aunt Lizabeth never forgave me. Sadly, she thought I'd stolen your Dad away from her. She seemed to forget the details. Unfortunately, I couldn't convince her that I'd never known she had feelings for your Dad. When she told me, years after we married, it was too late. I was upset, especially as she never loved anybody else. She never married."

Mum dropped a mountain of beans into a pan on the table and fumbled for a hanky to wipe away tears running down her pale cheeks.

"Sorry, Mum, I didn't mean to upset you." Jess changed the subject. She didn't want to rake up the past and asked, "Who looks younger, Mum, Fiona or me?" Looking at Fiona and pulling faces, she pretended to walk with a walking stick. "Let's help you finish preparing tea."

"All right, Jess, if you stop messing about and help Fiona peel the carrots and potatoes, I'll take the cheese out of the fridge for the cottage pie?"

"Great, you talk, we'll peel. We love your cottage pie, especially with extra strong cheese. When will Dad be home? I'm starving."

"Mum, your pies are awesome." Fiona joined in with praise for Mum.

Both sisters were thinking about the presence in the attic. They knew they had to return to sort out the packing cases full of memories and fusty old clothes. Mum was hoping to sell up and buy a small bungalow on the outskirts of the town but couldn't ask Dad to help. The doctor had warned them that Dad must take life easy. But there wasn't one prospective buyer amongst the crowd that invaded their home on Open Day. They were all complete time-wasters.

"Here's the cheese, Mum," said Jess. "I've grated it better than Fiona's worm-like pieces of cheese she did last week for the lasagne, haven't I?"

"It would be good if you didn't keep trying to be better than your sister, you're behaving like children. Stop it and let's get on with tea, next you'll be asking for fish fingers and Angel Delight! Do you think you'll be able to finish the attic stuff this weekend?"

They were distracted by a scraping noise upstairs.

"It sounds like dragging a body bag across the floor!" Jess said and the sisters looked at each other trying to look cool, a forced smile on their faces.

"Whatever's the matter with you girls? There are often strange, unexplained noises in this house. That's why I want a newer brighter house, minimal knick-knacks and less work faffing with dusting. This house has too many painful memories with Aunt Liz and what happened. But you two are jumpy today!"

Something or someone was noisily approaching the kitchen. They were all sitting bolt upright and waiting. The noises were getting louder. The old, creaky kitchen door opened, slowly and revealed...

"Dad, it's great to see you," said Fiona and Jess together as they lurched towards their Dad for a smothering hug. He grabbed the sisters and gave each of them a big kiss on Jess's then Fiona's cheek.

They'd expected something or someone else to open the kitchen door, maybe the ghost.

"Girls - but it was only last weekend when I saw you. You're more than usually pleased to see me," Dad said. "Have you girls been tidying the attic as promised?"

The sisters were quiet.

"Both of you lay the table while I go and put the peelings in the composter. Thanks for helping Mum with all the veg," said Dad.

"Whatever shall we do now, Jess?" Fiona whispered in Jess's ear.

"I'm going upstairs. If I'm not back in about twenty minutes, come looking for me, please?" said Jess.

"No, Silly! I'm coming with you," Fiona said as she followed closely behind.

Any brave feelings disappeared by the time they'd climbed the squeaky wooden stairs. As they turned the corner of the landing, they stopped. Fiona clung tightly to Jess's upper arm. The scraping noises had returned. Something was being dragged across the floor, two floors up. They dare not speak.

They both jumped. Something fell off the ceiling. It dropped on Jess's back and crawled down the low neckline of her pink blouse. Both sisters screamed, forgetting to be quiet as there might be somebody lurking in the attic.

"Somebody, something is attacking us, shh," Fiona whispered. "Jess, calm down, you baby. It won't hurt you; it's just a little spider. You stupid girl."

Jess tried to brush it off; it felt massive and it was on her bare neck. She shrieked again, and brushed something onto the floor... A third scream and Fiona couldn't help joining in as both sisters giggled hysterically...

With a sudden loud bang from downstairs, Mum shouted from the bottom of the stairs. "All right, girls? What's all the noise? Come down for tea this minute. Whatever's happening up there? Have you broken something?"

They looked into the blue painted attic room. The chair was back in its place against the back wall. Nothing looked disturbed. Fiona and Jess knew something had happened but couldn't explain what. Slowly, they went downstairs.

"Whatever was that noise?" asked Mum.

"It was a few photo albums falling over. Tell us more about Aunt Liz; tell us about your sister, will you? She always seemed a rather feisty, scary lady who had a past to hide." Jess giggled, nervously.

"Ignore baby Jess, Mum, she's ridiculous as usual. I need answers. Did Aunt Liz marry and have children?" asked Fiona as she fidgeted with a kitchen chair moving it backwards and forwards under the kitchen table.

"No, she never married. She always blamed me for her unhappiness. I always loved my older sister. I wanted to look after her, but she wouldn't let me and always bore a grudge," said Mum, choking back the tears welling in her sad, dark green eyes.

At that moment, there was a huge bang from upstairs. Fiona and Jess jumped. Fiona knocked over the chair she was standing behind.

Everybody stood still. Dad was the first to speak.

"Come along, it must be something the girls moved in the attic that's fallen on the floor," Dad snapped. "Nothing more sinister than that, I'm sure. I'll go and see what it is." He stopped in the doorway. "Anybody like to come with me?"

"I'll come but only if Jess comes with us!" said Fiona.

The sisters looked at each other. "Ok," said Jess. "Let's go."

When they arrived in the blue room there was Cuddles, their large, well-fed ginger cat looking sheepish, cowering under that chair involved in the happening. She'd knocked Aunt Liz's favourite yellow flowery vase off the sideboard. Bits of the yellow china littered the floor. The cat shot past them and fled downstairs.

"I knew it was Cuddles," said Jess.

"No you didn't. You didn't have a clue. You're never right, silly," Fiona answered back.

"Stop it, girls. Your dad and I've had enough. Act your ages. You're fifty-seven and fifty-nine, not seven and nine! Behave like it," said Mum.

Kate A Harris

October 2

The Seminar

As part of my undergraduate degree at Edinburgh University, I decided to take Politics only on the assumption that I'd be in Henry Drucker's' seminar. He *was* the Politics Department at Edinburgh, with an allegedly huge personality and a strong presence on BBC Scotland at election time. He was the main reason that most students chose to study Politics at Edinburgh.

We had to queue up to sign for the seminars and, after a lot of pushing and shoving, I got to the noticeboard only to see that I was number 32 on the list of 8 attendees for his weekly seminar.

Undeterred I pushed my way back out of the crowd and trotted round to the Politics Department, a tall dark stoned house set back off a cobbled street. I knocked on the austere black door and waited. I still felt as though I was being watched. There didn't seem to be any intercom system or camera but I still felt watched as I stood there. No sounds came from within and I finally found a bell and pressed it, moving back onto the cold Edinburgh granite step. I waited.

Finally, after what seemed like an excessively long and conspicuous wait, the door creaked and a short, squat janitor opened the door. I found myself checking the brass plaque to see if this really was the Politics Department as the expression on his face implied they got very few visitors.

'I need to see Henry Drucker's' secretary,' I said, before he could decide to shut the door on me.

'Follow me,' he said as he led me up the dark narrow stairs, past many doors adorned with professors' names. It was so quiet and deserted, I really wasn't at all sure I was in the right place.

It was clearly coffee time when we finally reached the secretaries' office. The room was small and warm and the atmosphere relaxed and informal. The janitor introduced me to the lady seated behind the desk nearest to the door, before helping himself to the tea and biscuits the secretaries were sharing.

I took a deep breath in and began my speech.

'I need your help,' I said, before a long pause which might well have been mistaken for dramatic effect but, in truth, I wasn't sure what to say next. The secretary smiled kindly at me.

'I only came to Edinburgh because of Henry Drucker. He's the reason I'm here and, sadly, due to the mad crush around the seminar lists, I've not managed to get into his seminar. Can you help me? I really, really want to be in his session.'

She smiled at me over her glasses.

'His seminars are always in demand but all of our professors here at Edinburgh are highly rated. Have you thought about Professor Waldon?'

'Professor Waldon isn't Henry Drucker. Henry Drucker is inspirational, he is a thought leader here in Scotland and I know he'll push me to the limits of political knowledge. I love how he challenges the status quo and persuades in that kindly-killer sort of way. I *need* to be in his seminar. Politics won't be worth taking if I can't be in it.'

I'd given it my best shot. After a few moments of silence, she glanced behind me to her colleagues and I thought she was looking for some guidance. I turned around to see a collection of smiling faces looking at me. There was no sense of urgency about them but it was hard to tell if my argument was winning them over. The janitor was listening too, sat back with his arms folded behind his head, swinging on the chair with one leg crossed over the other. Their smiles gave me the boost I needed to go in once more.

'My life won't be worth living if I don't get onto that webinar,' I wailed, instantly regretting the words as soon as I saw the expression on the kindly secretary's face shift from warm to irritated. I knew I had gone too far.

'I'm sorry,' she said. 'I really can recommend any of the professors here and you'll still get to see Professor Drucker in the lectures each week.'

'But lectures aren't seminars,' I said, surprising myself as the words continued to come out. 'Is there no way at all you could find of slipping me into his seminar?'

'Now if I did that, how unfair would it be to the others who also queued?'

'Yes, but I can assure you none of the others are as desperate as I am to be in his seminar. I only came to Edinburgh to be inspired by him.'

A well-groomed eyebrow raised from behind her glasses and she started to move some papers on her desk. Knowing I was beaten, I left the room, somewhat embarrassed but still remembering to thank them for their time. I took one more look at the kindly smiling faces, even the janitor looked sympathetic.

I saw myself out of the building and trudged head down back outside onto the cobbled street where it had started to drizzle.

A week later, signed up for Professor Waldon's seminar, I sat waiting for the first Politics lecture of the term. The room was buzzing with anticipation as 200 first year students eagerly awaited the arrival of Professor Drucker who was going to be speaking on the subject of Quangos. The door opened and the lecture hall fell silent as he entered the room.

I watched in sheer amazement as the janitor took to the podium and began to speak.

Fiona White

October 3

Missing

William Gray watched as one of the biggest and safest ships in the world began its maiden voyage. People waved and cheered from the quay, balloons were released into the air and tugboats hooted as they slowly led R.M.S Titanic from the quayside.

"America, an opportunity of a lifetime!" his wife Mabel had stated. William had promised to send for her as soon as he found work and somewhere for them to live, which he had no intention of doing. He'd said goodbye to Mabel and left to catch the bus to Southampton.

As passengers, in all their finery, waved goodbye and blew kisses to friends and loved ones on the quay, William Gray watched his opportunity to escape to a better and happier life - without a wife who took pleasure in making him miserable - sail into the distance along with his self-respect.

He cuffed tears from his eyes. His heart sank. He needed time to think. He picked up his suitcase and turned his back on what his wife had said was his last chance to make something of himself. He took a deep breath. He didn't want to live in America. He liked England. He liked Hampshire. Smiling, William recalled many happy holidays he had with his parents in Southampton as a child. It was then that he decided he was not going home straight away.

It would take the Titanic six days to get to New York. It would take William a week to find a job, and another week, at least, to find somewhere for him and Mabel to live. William slipped his hand inside the top of his overcoat, felt his wallet, and laughed. He had enough money to last him three weeks in Southampton. April was not the holiday season, so there would be cheap lodgings for him to have a well-deserved and peaceful holiday. Besides, he could not face the tongue-lashing he knew his wife would give him if he went home. He shuddered. She would mock him and make his life miserable. If he told her the truth and said he didn't want to live in America, she would say he was weak and had no backbone. If he lied, said he had missed the ship through no fault of his own, she would say he was stupid, shout at him and call him a grey man. "Grey and dull like your name!" She enjoyed making him feel small.

Thank goodness he had his savings safely tucked away. A few weeks, three at the most, was all he needed. By then, William hoped he would know what to do with the rest of his life.

Madalyn Morgan

October 4

A New Beginning?

So far, so good. As Chief Medical Officer aboard Pioneer 37 of the Scatterseed mission, it was planned that I would be the first to be roused. And here I am, awake and fully functioning it would seem, but totally alone on just one of the vast hibernation decks. Soon I shall begin the re-awakening process, starting with the full medical team, who will then oversee bringing the 5,000 migrants on board back to life. But for now, I will allow myself a short, solitary reflection on the planet I used to call home.

How did we reach the point where, not only human life, but nearly all plant and animal life, became unsustainable? Why did we not heed decades of warnings? Why did we ignore and often dismiss growing evidence as our environment degraded at an ever increasing pace? Of course, over the latter part of what we knew as the 21st century, there was increasing concern, then desperation, and finally mass panic and chaos. But we had left it all too late. This was not due to a lack of ingenuity, or technology, or even finance; no, our failure was the inability to co-operate, to reach out, to consider others. Humankind polarised, fragmented. We built walls, formed self-serving pacts, harboured false suspicion, hurled spiteful accusations at opposing alliances.

And those who were powerful and wealthy enough began to plan their escape. It was plain that Earth was entering its Autumn; a harsh and final Winter would follow. Thousands of pioneering explorers would seek out and inhabit new worlds. Or was this tiny percentage of the human population just another group of desperate refugees? From the dawning of the 22nd century, fleets of huge inter-galactic life-rafts, fifty from the Western Democratic Alliance alone, were abandoning Mother Earth.

Such a sad and desperate plan. Many of the first escaping craft were shot down by enemy missiles before they had even escaped Earth's atmosphere. And doubtless, many more are marooned in the vast, unknown and lonely cosmos, never to reach their intended destinations. And what of the millions who were left on the dying Earth? I don't suppose we will ever know their unthinkable fate.

Pioneer 37 is now orbiting Exo-planet 4398z, seven light years from Earth. The universe has been seeded; the human species has been given a second chance. For me, one question remains, lurking in the dark, shadowy recesses of my conscience: are we even deserving of a new beginning?

Steve Redshaw

October 5

The Box

The box moves. I'm sure it moved - but I am sitting on a bus, over the wheel, the back left hand one, my favourite seat. From there I can see the road ahead; anticipating direction is the only way I can cope with the sick-making twists and turns of travel. The box on my lap is the standard design issued by 'Companion Animal Supplies' - a uniformly matt black. Far too chic, especially with its gold lettering of 'Fur, Feather & Fin' repeated as a pattern around the top just below the shiny black tape that seals the lid. Pretentious. It's only cardboard after all. Below the tape is a row of tiny perforations which make it a multi-purpose carrier for live or never-been-alive stuff. I know if I peer in I'll see nothing, and despite my hope, if I could, I'd see nothing that moves.

A fading hope makes me sniff the holes. Nothing animal. No furry kitten or puppy then. As if!

"You mustn't shake it," he'd warned, "and carry it carefully. Don't let it drop suddenly – or at all. Just take this receipt to the collection point and wait while they pack it up." And I do as I am told, collect it and make for home.

My stop is approaching. I can't reach the buzzer across the gangway without tilting the box, so I have to arch back to press the button on the pole behind me. My stomach pushes the box forward and I smack my left arm around it so it can't tilt forward. I continue to hold it carefully against me, left arm around it, chin clamped on top. The other hand goes out to clutch a succession of poles as I make my way to the front. Somehow I manage to glance down to detect the hazard of sprawling legs. I must not drop and break this his latest treasure, some splendid underwater palace, no doubt, for that aquarium of his. It's taken over one whole side of what was once our best room. We had to have the floor reinforced. My comfortable room. Ruined.

The bus stops and I step off carefully. Give the driver an emphatic 'thank you' to let him know I'm on terra firma. I avoid the grass. Mustn't slip now and drop it. Tempting though. A short careful walk home, box lowered with care while key inserted in lock. Box taken into kitchen. Placed on table. His present to me. This time, though, it's not for my birthday, which he never forgets. My friends think it's so considerate of him, "You're so lucky," and I go along with it. Keep up appearances.

"Don't open it before I get back." He was quite emphatic. Soon I'll have to admire this unbirthday surprise for me, some gaudy Disney-like concoction of conical roofs and gaping arches for his little gaping-mouthed finny friends to flip through. Little staring eyes that he stares back at. Little round mouths opening, shutting, gobbing out stones, or just gobbing. Sometimes I imagine he's trying to lip read them.

I wonder if I could knit myself a sort of mermaid's tail, put on a wig and sit in it braless. Would he actually notice me then? If I inhabited this monstrosity he'll claim he bought for me? Yet he's never even noticed I've retreated to the kitchen. To my favourite box. The one that speaks to me, both meanings, literal and metaphorical. Don't know why people grumble about TV – they should try watching Endless Aquarium. He never calls it TV, or the telly. It's always 'the television'. He's the punctilious sort. Very precise. And as cold as a bloody fish.

"Don't open it." Huh, hasn't the man ever heard of Pandora? Not unless it's some sort of octopus. I stare at it. I don't even bother to get a knife. My nail's strong enough to press through the tape where the lid meets the box. I do it carefully, so I can replace it later. He'll never notice. But I can't have been careful enough. Along the third side a faint shush-shushing noise alerts me – oops, I've torn it – in both senses of the word. My nail must have got blunt, but I can't stop now. I'll fix it later. I risk it tearing again, and blithely ignore the shushing, ripping sound. I briskly slide my thumb along the last side. Smiling with rebellion, I snatch the lid off, brush my hair away from my eyes, lean over and peer in. That shushing again. A small eye, round like a berry, unblinking, rises to meet me and a tiny black tongue, flickering. Forked.

Chris Rowe

October 6

On The Carpet

'It's a good story, but I don't believe a word of it.'

My heart sank into my boots and oozed out through the holes.

'And you had better fasten those laces or you will be in sick bay with broken noses.' We bent down to fasten them, all thumbs, especially Philip. I have to tie his.

'Not now! I haven't finished talking to you.'

We stood up again, waiting for the worst. A hundred lines at best. Or a letter to our parents. That would mean no footie in the park with Dad on Saturday. Or they might take Philip away. Please, God, not that.

'I am sure that you are aware of the rules of this school. But you seem not to understand that the rules apply to all pupils, including you. It appears that you have broken at least three rules, and not the least is honesty. Not only have you been absent from school without a valid reason; not only has our excellent caretaker, Mr. Brandon, discovered you playing by the river, but you, James, have told me a pack of lies so inventive that you will probably end up scriptwriting for commercial television.'

Wow, scriptwriting! I could be famous! I could write *Doctor Who*. I'd be good at that. So there they are, the Doctor and Philip, surrounded by Daleks, about to be exterminated. Yer! And one Dalek takes Philip and another Dalek takes the Doctor and they drag them off to the Blotherpang all covered with green slime and one eye that rotates so it can see in all directions. And they tie them up, no, they put magic on them so they can't move, and the Blatherpang comes towards the Doctor with his turbo jet exterminator and says...

'Are you listening to me? James, I am talking to you. Yes, you. Or are you up there in the clouds?'

'Yes, Sir. I mean Miss. I mean Mrs. Withers, Miss.'

'I cannot allow you to continue with this disregard for the ethos we have in our school, which you are both doing your utmost to bring into disrepute. Now, perhaps you would be so kind as to explain exactly and truthfully why you chose to play by the river rather than attend lessons, so causing Mr. Brandon to waste his free time to escort you to school. You first, James.'

The Doctor showed no fear, even though he was quaking inside. He had faced monsters before but now here was a problem. How could he explain that they were on the planet Zetarix in order to exterminate the Blotherpang that was threatening to destroy the Earth?

'I do not have all day, James. Perhaps it would be better if I asked your twin. Philip...'

No, she mustn't ask Philip. Philip's eyes had gone all glassy. I had to get him out of here or he would have one of his fits.

'No, Miss, Mrs. Withers, Miss. Don't ask him, Miss, I'll tell you. It was like this, Miss. I had to look after my Mum because she isn't very well, and then get Philip ready, then wash up because my dad had gone to the job shop again, so we had to run, and we were on our way to school and we had just got to the bridge when we saw this Dalek, this dog, in the river and it was splashing about as if it was in trouble, see, so we thought we had better go and save the Earth, the dog, and we went down and rescued it and it shook green slime all over us and said, 'I am going to exterminate you.' No, that was the Blatherpang, I mean Mr Brandon, and he said, 'I have had it up to here with you two. I am going to report you to the headmistress and with a bit of luck you will be exterminated,' I mean expelled. And he grabbed me by the collar and held Philip's arm and brought us to school.'

'As I said before, James, It's a good story, but I don't believe a word of it. If this happens again, I shall contact your parents, and I don't want to have to do that with the problems they have. But, you, James, are supposed to look after your brother, not get him into danger. Now, go to your classroom. You have already missed most of the morning. Oh, and for extra homework tonight, I would like you to write a three page story entitled, *How I Saved the Earth*, and bring it to me before assembly.'

Wendy Goulstone

October 7

Field Of Vision

It was perhaps 1997. We were at Glastonbury Festival. We went as a group in a hired minibus sharing the cost, and our friend Adam driving because he isn't a drinker - very useful in a friend. We managed to cram all the camping equipment between the seats. This wasn't our first festival and we all loved it. Glastonbury to my mind is the first and best because it is spread over a vast area run by very experienced organisers. It raises vast amounts of money for charities, CND, Greenpeace and so on. There are many areas of entertainment, a huge comedy tent and a full circus. The whole green fields area is full of alternative healing and set round ancient standing stones.

There are three main music stages with many more alternative music sites too. The main stage is built on a lovely sloping field, meaning one can see the stage from the very back of the field and there are huge viewing screens either side of the stage too. There are paths filled with every kind of food you could imagine, coffee shops, clothes stalls, beer tents, cider buses, and camping equipment stalls in case you camped in the wrong place and your tent blew away. And not to mention hundreds of portaloos in different areas.

All the roads are thronged with hundreds of people all going in different directions to different areas. One hundred thousand happy folk thronging the paths. All around this are fields crammed with little and big tents where we all go to sleep eventually. Mind you, things keep going 24 hours because it is midsummer. In the dark and being only five foot tall and with no sense of direction, I hold onto the person in front of me always.

We had a camp place up the hill and under a pylon. It wasn't just the music, the people, the smells, it was being with a group of friends and family too. On this our third day, we went to the main stage and wound our way in amongst the crowd to a place in the middle to wait for a band we wanted to see, maybe REM. By looking to my left I had a good view of the circle of portaloos. In front was parked a fire truck with six firefighters on its roof watching the show. I decided if I used that as my marker I could get there and back on my own. I told my group and set off full of confidence but when I came out my fire truck had left!

I tried not to panic and started to thread my way back in but of course on each day we had been either further up the field or down! Now I was panicking and pinning my mind on my willing husband to feel my panic and come get me, but it was my daughter who picked up my vibes and came and called me in. I was so relieved, I cried. Everyone else fell about laughing.

Ruth Hughes

October 8

Foreign Food

The sun was sinking towards the horizon, but was taking its time about it. The sky was clear, and there was barely a breath of a gentle breeze occasionally moving the marram grass on the dunes, and the sea-thrift on the cliff. The long sandy beach was completely empty. No wildlife digging about for a last snack before dark. Not even a seagull. There was no sound, no bird cries, no rustling of vegetation, no sound of waves breaking on the shore, or drawing back again. Hushed, everything was hushed, that was the word for it. Almost expectant.

Sylvie stood motionless in the wide gap between two tall dunes, where the duckboard gave way to the sand, and took it all in. She could sense, rather than hear, Yves as he came up behind her. She turned to smile at him.

The ultra-bright flash was blinding. Colour was bleached from everything. Disoriented, she made a grab for Yves, and he for her. The burning, blinding flash was nothing compared to the horrendous noise that followed. A loud, deafening, bang to outdo any noise ever heard before, and the pressure wave that hit next threw their unconscious bodies to the ground, way back behind the lines of dunes. Sand and seawater covered them, but they were unaware of this, and of everything, for many weeks to come.

+ +

Sylvie opened her eyes slowly, but only because the strange clicking noise, that had come to her attention first, appeared to be getting closer, and she couldn't identify it. The light burned and she let out an involuntary cry, but it was a noise she had never heard before, not from man nor beast. Her eyes had clamped shut, leaving her only with hearing to keep her connected to the world outside her body, which she then tried to move, and found she couldn't. She could not move any part of it, or feel anything touching it. In desperation she made that awful noise again.

A chiming sort of voice said, "Sleep. Don't struggle. Sleep", and the clicking noise started up again, moving away. Again Sylvie struggled to move any part of her, but in vain. Exhausted she drifted off.

She woke to total silence, but trying to lift her eyelids confirmed it was still too bright, wherever she was, and once more her attempt to move her body was fruitless. She couldn't move her head, but could open her mouth a little. She sucked in the air. It tasted different, but had a hint of something familiar. She just couldn't place it. Why was thinking so tiring? Why couldn't she move or feel anything? Where was Yves?

She tried to call, but just that awful noise issued from the back of her throat. The clicking noise started again, and this time it came very close. Very, very close. The chiming voice came once more. "Don't struggle. Save energy. I will give you something to help you sleep." Sylvie wanted to say NO, she tried to say NO, but a sudden wave of cold shot through her, numbing her thought processes. It was scented strongly with something she tried to identify, thought she knew. Aniseed?

When she woke for the third time the light was considerably less bright, and she could hold her eyes open for longer. Hovering above her face was an arrangement of gleaming metal bars and tubes that snaked outside her limited range of vision. With immense effort she found she was able to move her eyes left or right. Then she wished she hadn't tried, for standing close by her head was a blue-metal cylinder, that appeared to be connecting a flask to one of the tubes. The cylinder was ringed with flashing lights, and near the top were six orbs that could only be described as eyes. The cylinder moved. So that was the clicking noise. Sylvie tried her voice again and found she could now make a softer noise. In response, the chiming voice issued from the cylinder. "You will soon be whole. Sleeping is good."

The last time Sylvie woke up she could see straight away that her position had changed. She was now standing upright. Or hanging maybe? She seemed to be swaying gently. She could see quite well now, and found herself watching two of the blue cylinders scooting backwards and forwards between several platforms, or tables, on which grey wrapped bodies lay. More cylinders came, and went, or stayed. They were apparently tending the bodies, and Sylvie knew she had been one of them not long back. The chiming voice kept repeating the reassuring phrases, and sounded exactly the same no matter which cylinder was talking.

It was only now that she began to question where she was. She was looking at technical expertise that she had never seen, or heard of, before. She wanted to ask about everything, and tested her voice, but it was still not there, just the softer version of the guttural noise as before. She initially thought of the cylinders as just machines, but after a while realised they discussed between themselves, and even gave the impression that they were just chatting at times. She was fascinated with their comings and goings, the changing patterns of the flashing lights, that seemed reproduced in all of them, at some point or other. Like a code, or part of a different communication system. Her concentration started to drift away.

It was pulled back into sharp focus when a cylinder started to move one of the beds across the room to where she was standing. As it drew alongside Sylvie could see that the grey wrapping wasn't like a blanket. It wasn't soft, but hard, and looked more like a rigid fibreglass cocoon. The cylinder gripped the cocoon, lifted it, and literally hung it up next to her, by the huge metal hook protruding from the back of the all too human head. Yves!

Sylvie was appalled. Yet she couldn't even feel sick, as her body was still totally numb, as if not there at all. The cylinder nudged her along, and then moved Yves, making room to hang another body. Then another, and another. With each move a tunnel mouth in the wall crept closer. What was coming next? What was going on?

What happened next was a rapid descent in the dark, at quite a sharp angle, until she emerged in a huge, dim room. There was a jolt as she slipped off the rail she'd been hanging from, and got picked up on a hook on a moving belt high above. Yves' cocoon hung so close to her that she could almost kiss him. As she moved through the room she could see more tunnel mouths disgorging, in turn, more cocoons. All with human heads. The only noise was the clanking of the belt collecting up the cocoons' hooks. No doubt about it, this was a storage system. They were being warehoused! Her cocoon passed through a wall of grey mist.

Sterilised and frozen, for Sylvie, time stood still.

+   +

Who knows how much time passed before she, and others, were moved out of the warehouse and thawed out, but for them it was no time at all after passing through the mist curtain. As awareness returned they realised the soft voice they could hear was speaking English, of a sort, and repeating the message over and over again.

"It is only right to know how you are here. We have taken your world and it is no more. You have been restored and fattened. Today you will be at our table."

Several cocoons were dropped into a huge container, which then moved them forward into a room where many creatures sat, hunched over low tables. These new overlords, neither insect nor mollusc, but a revolting combination of both, with a healthy dose of total alien thrown in the mix, were eating. Two cocoons were left in front of each alien.

Sylvie's last sight was Yves' head bouncing across the floor by the next table. Then the alien at her table ripped off her head, and began to consume the liquidised contents of the cocoon, breaking it open with huge mandibles, to lick out every tasty bit with its long, rough tongue. Then it signalled for a third cocoon.

That's the trouble with foreign food, it never fills you up for long.

EE Blythe

October 9

A New Beginning

Saffran and Inuelas flew down the starlight corridor, their ethereal wings enabling them to move at some speed. Saffran noted the turning of the corridor and guided Inuelas safely around it. Inuelas had lost his sight as the result of a stray supernova erupting at the battle of the seven stars. The void between the void had burned that day.

Swiftly the pair flew on twisting through the maze of nebulous gasses and diving deep into the vortex of swirling black. Even their pursuers would hesitate before plunging into the inky whirlpool. Saffran breathed a sigh of relief as they were pulled into the vanishing point and reappeared on the other side. Her faith proved true.

Travelling at the speed of time they put aeons behind them and witnessed the birth of a billion galaxies in the blink of an eye. Saffran worried that their pursuers would catch up to them but a sneaky glance with her tail set her mind at ease. They had not come through, perhaps believing that the pair had met oblivion.

Inuelas faltered and his wings clipped the shadow matter debris; he winced in pain as the shadows erupted into anti-light and surged forward to consume the very stars that had recently come into being. They wept for the loss of that beautiful canvas of creation, seeing all that was left was a flaming chunk of iron.

Saffran gasped in astonishment as she observed their tears being pulled into the fiery ferrous mass spinning speedily amidst the hissing steam and settling finally into a sphere of water and land. Taking Inuelas by the hand she led him down, alighting on the crystal beach, their footsteps causing the crystals to shatter into a fine carpet of sand.

At the water's edge Saffran kissed Inuelas' cheek and plunged a fiery claw into his already hollow heart. The sound of his dying moments became the rush of the wind and the thunder in the skies as Saffran retrieved the glowing orb from his chest and lowered it into the sea.

The orb dispersed in a sudden bang of epic proportions, infesting every corner of the sphere with emerging life. As she lay down next to her dead companion, her final happy thoughts were that at least here, away from the darkness, life can start again.

Christopher Trezise

October 10

The Saga Of The Ashes

Iris had requested that her ashes should be scattered at Morecambe Bay after her death. This was where she had been happiest, where she had been evacuated during the war, It doesn't say much for her home life does it? The executor of her will asked her brother-in-law and his son to do the deed. They live at Preston which is not far away. They agreed and were given a sum of money for train fare and meals.

The box that held the ashes was beautifully decorated, exactly like the coffin - green grass, beautiful green trees and a black and white cat.

When they arrived at Morecambe, the tide was right up to a little fence at the side of the road. For some reason, the ex-son-in-law thought she had requested to be poured into the sea. It would have been much easier to scatter her on the beach, but no!

So, climbing over the little fence into the sea, what he didn't realise is that there were rocks under the water and they had slippy seaweed on them. He slipped off one and was up to his knees. He turned to warn the son but he was too late. The son slipped and grazed his thigh. It bled.

When they had got their balance back, they emptied the box. When they had finally fulfilled Iris's wishes, they journeyed home again.

I must admit that, when I heard their story, I had a job not to smile. I do think that Iris had the last laugh.

Ruth Hughes

October 11

Linden Yle

A young man was closing the town's library doors at eight o'clock that spring night.

Adam was a young fit man who enjoyed football and went to the gym regularly. He never stood a chance. One unlucky day, he found a spot on his forearm, quite large, the size of a little finger nail but green, the colour of a dandelion leaf.

Next day, when the spot was the size of a thumbnail, he went to the doctor, who was not impressed: "This has gone septic. You need to put some TCP on it." The doctor bandaged the arm and sent him straight home.

The next day brought another shift at the main desk but Adam could not move his arm and had to phone in sick. Only ten am, he could not keep his eyes open and staggered to bed.

Next morning, a strange voice woke Adam: "Good morning Adam, can you hear me?"

"What's that voice? Who's there? What's going on?"

Adam's bedroom was deserted but he could not move below the neck.

"Critical mass reached. Now we can control your auditory nerve. Adam, your body has incubated us very well. Thank you very much."

"Come on! Who said that?" He was baffled, helpless and anxious. "Where are you?"

"Look at your arm, Adam."

He cast his eyes down with difficulty. The spot was the size of half a cricket ball.

"Congratulations," said the disembodied voice. "You are the first successful subject of our invasion."

"What are you talking about? Why can't I see you? How long...?"

"You can see where we live, Adam. In that spot on your arm. We are

Yle, not germs. We are alien spores if your xenobiologists had to classify us. Your very healthy physique is the perfect environment for Yle to reproduce."

Adam said, "This is some sort of trick. Ian?

"The Yle have been here 2,500 years. We know everything about you."

"Are you spies? Working for Putin?"

"Typical humanity," said the disembodied voice, "always expecting bigger threats, enormous challenges, leviathans, a colossus or Godzilla, King Kong, global climate change; even your deity has to be immense whereas our civilization could fit in a suitcase. Nothing personal, Adam, to the Yle you are a... human resource."

The story doesn't end well for Adam .

Police in the town were suddenly very busy that week and took a while to find Adam's body but he squelched into the body bag very easily.

Later Emma, the pathologist, stared into Adam's cactus opaque dead eyes and made the classic diagonal post-mortem cuts. She only revealed a bag of bones surrounded by watermelon green mash and a rodent cage smell.

That night, she missed her aerobics class with weird spots somewhere very sensitive and was off sick the next day.

Many of the users of the town library were disturbed by the condition of the books that month and particularly found the seaweed green mould very distressing.

Chris Wright

October 12

Time To Wait

The storm raged above the deserted railway station, rain lashing down, thunder rumbling away like distant guns. The whole sky lit up when a huge bolt of lightning flashed across the horizon and speared the ground.

As the Bristol Express approached, the driver was distracted by the storm and thought he saw a red light. He applied the brakes in a hurry and the train stopped abruptly, jolting Charlie awake. Still half-asleep, he picked up his briefcase and jumped out of the carriage, slamming the door behind him. Immediately the express started to move. As it gathered speed, Charlie saw by the reflected light of the passing carriages the boarded up windows and the empty platform of an abandoned station.

To Charlie, alone in the dark, watching the angry lightning and listening to the heavy thunder, it felt as if he were standing in the middle of an old black and white war movie. He sighed and moved further under cover, away from the unrelenting rain.

How could he have been so bloody stupid? Any fool could've seen this station had been closed for years. He took out his phone to call Jenna to come and fetch him. She would not be best pleased coming out on a night like this.

There was no signal. The storm was passing and the rain was slackening off. Charlie's eyes had become accustomed to the darkness, and he looked around, hoping for a payphone. The station clock was still going, odd that, and the hands stood at eight forty-five. There was, of course, no payphone. And even more stupid of him to expect one on a disused railway station.

He glanced at the clock again and rubbed his eyes. Ten thirty. He looked at his watch, an expensive one that could tell the time under water or on top of Mount Everest. Eight forty-seven. He shook his head;

the clock couldn't possibly be working after all this time. It was a trick of the light, the darkness or the bad weather. To prove his point, lightning flashed overhead and showed him a clock with no hands.

Picking up his briefcase, he started walking towards the end of the platform, hoping to find a way out.

A voice behind him spoke. 'Excuse me, sir, passengers are not allowed beyond this point.'

Relief rushed through Charlie's veins. He was not going to be stuck here all night. He turned round and saw a man wearing a uniform and a peaked cap with the words "Station Master" on it. The man had long mutton chop whiskers and he stood beneath one of the flickering gas mantels, consulting his pocket watch.

'Am I glad to see you!' Charlie said. 'I thought this station was closed. I got off here by mistake.'

He stopped. There'd been no lights a moment ago. But gas lamps? In 2022? He saw the benches, the porter's trolley, the troughs planted with spring flowers closed against the night. He spun round. The windows were no longer boarded up and he saw an empty waiting room where a welcoming fire blazed.

The Station Master put his pocket watch away. 'Come along, sir. Mind the edge.'

Bewilderment was turning to panic. His heart beat faster and his mouth was dry. He swallowed and his voice came out in a croak.

'What's going on here? Who are you?'

'I am the Station Master, sir.'

'When's the next train?' Charlie asked. He was afraid to hear the answer, yet knew he had to ask.

'Oh, there won't be a next train for you, sir. You will be staying here – with us. We've been waiting for someone new.'

'Is some has-been comedian going to jump and shout "Surprise!"?' Charlie said. 'This is one of those prank the public TV programmes? A Hallowe'en special?'

It was the only logical explanation he could think of: that he had been the victim of some horrible practical joke.

'Take your time, sir. You have plenty. Come inside and meet everyone.'

Behind the Station Master, the waiting room was full of people, despairing faces pressed against the window panes.

Charlie saw and he understood and he wept.

Fran Neatherway

October 13

Just Another Day?

An extract from my diary - Thursday, October 13, 2022

7 am. Day began as normal. Kind husband delivered welcome hot cuppa, my favourite antioxidant Red Bush, South African Rooibos tea. Reminded me of wonderful holidays in South Africa, visits to elder sister in Johannesburg. She'll be basking in baking hot 30+ degrees. Lovely. Listened to radio and read few a pages, The Thursday Murder Club. Didn't want to enjoy, but did. Great story, plot, funny and escapism.

8 am. Got up, went downstairs, opened blinds and curtains, showered, daily ablutions etc.

8.30 am. Breakfast, porridge with local honey, cherry yoghurt. Filling. Boring jobs, dry day, clothes into washer, switched on, hang outside later.

9.15 am. Visited Homebase, purchased bedding plants for colourful hanging baskets, front of house through dull winter months, replacing still blooming beautiful begonias, bright yellows and fruity oranges. Pansies, primroses and primulas front and back garden. And batteries for torches, power cuts? Peter returned home. I shopped. The Range exchanged third cousin Harris's age seven card for eight! Naomi not contacted for a couple of years! Answered yesterday. Ring Saturday, Harris's birthday.

12 pm. Decided to walk home. Dilemma. No bus pass, nor cash! An adventure, walked different way, first time. On tow path fella told me bridge nearby. Wrong. Half a mile+, needed to be other side of canal. Ended up at Clifton Cruisers and The Canal Lounge at Bridge 66 café. First time. Will return. Very friendly couple. No gluten free goodies to revitalise. Enjoyed cuppa tea and view, canal and boats. Long pleasant walk home. Miles out of way. Luckily found quicker way home.

12.50 pm. Washing hung outside. Lunch, toast, satsuma, choc bar, water. Tired, watched telly, Mary Rose recording. Forty years since lifted from Solent. Great memories, watched with Mother from round tower, Southsea. Funny, Howard Doris name of lifting cradle. Watched from harbour as slid past on back of ship, 8.10 pm. Dark, eerie, few lights casting shadows on wreck. Must return to Museum again soon.

3 pm. On computer, emails. Barnardo book contact's epistle 1959, aged thirteen, St. John's Ambulance to 1966. NNEB qualified. Written history, Head Office, answered queries, interesting, lots unusable! Most prolific contact. Washing into conservatory.

6.40 pm. Dinner, Peter cooked: full salad, pan fried chicken, mayonnaise potatoes. Watched Emmerdale, emotional, Faith died. Returned to computer. Forty-three Nat West Bank Branches closing. Sad, including my first bank, Palmerston Road, Southsea, over fifty years ago. Wrote this. Bed.

Kate A Harris

October 14

Presentation

I pulled into a space right outside the office and I took a breath. I was nervous, but I was so ready for this. I looked over to the passenger seat to grab my things, when I suddenly realised I'd forgotten my notebook. Damn it!

Never mind, I had my laptop and I had the presentation. That was the main thing.

I stepped out of the car and quickly noticed how eerily quiet it was. There were meant to be over a hundred people here to listen to my talk. In fact, the office looked empty.

"Oh God!" I shouted as I realised that I was at the wrong place. The presentation was being held at HQ, right across the other side of town.

I swiftly leapt back into my car and I started the engine.

I couldn't be late. I was doing the talk. They were all coming to see me!

Edging over the speed limit, I hurtled down some main roads, but I soon ground to a halt in the peak time traffic.

This was no good. What was I going to say?

An idea hit me.

As soon as the traffic started to move, I cut down a side road and headed for the countryside. The quiet country lanes might be a long way round, but if I kept moving it would certainly be quicker at this time of day.

I overtook a tractor, skidded past two cyclists and then whizzed down a single track road.

I saw up ahead two cars had pulled in to let a van through. There was no room for me. I'd have to reverse.

I was not good at reversing. I stopped the car, looked behind me, attempted to reverse in a straight line, when I found myself going straight through a fence and into a field.

Rather than look like an idiot, I decided to commit, and I headed on across the bumpy grassland. As much as I was scaring the sheep, it was saving me a good ten minutes.

I had to hit another fence to re-join the road, but now I was just one minute away from my destination. I'd worry about the damage later.

I screeched into the very busy car park, ditched my rather battered car, and I raced inside. Huffing at the door, I said my hellos to my colleagues. I then raced back to my car to fetch my laptop bag. I finally caught my breath as I stood at the lectern, now fifteen minutes behind schedule, and I pressed for the presentation to begin.

"Good morning everyone," I began, forcing a smile onto my face. "Thank you for being here. Today I'll be sharing my top twenty tips for a more organised life."

Lindsay Woodward

October 15

Swap Shop Or Tiswas

If I were to watch most of the television programmes from the 1970s again, they would probably be very cheesy and very disappointing. A while back I saw an episode of *The Dukes of Hazard* and it was terrible. But at the time, all of these shows seemed magnificent and exciting, especially the American imports which opened us up to a whole new world of thrilling drama.

Remember, we had only three channels - BBC1, BBC2 and ITV - and even these did not broadcast all day, and certainly not all night. Until 1976, we had a black and white television screen, only to be replaced by a rental colour set around the time of the Olympic games that year. The delivery man stopped to watch a key race, I seem to recall. A shop in the town centre called Multi-Broadcast was the source of our television rentals. The set was voluminous, though not much of this was taken up by the screen which only extended to about 22 inches. This box, though, was the main source of our entertainment and we watched it far too much. If it broke down, it was a tragedy. We sat around staring at the dulled screen, anxiously waiting for the repairman to arrive. He would remove the back panel with his screwdriver and often replace a key part which had burnt out. Sometimes, he would have to give us a replacement set from his van. Then, the joy of being able to watch again - our window on the world restored at last.

Saturday mornings were key watching times. Since 1974, I had been treated to *Tiswas* (standing for 'today is Saturday, watch and smile'), the anarchic ITV show fronted by Chris Tarrant and featuring, among others, a young Lenny Henry, continuity presenter Peter Tomlinson as *Tarzan*, and Sally James. There was something delightfully chaotic and under rehearsed about the whole thing and I loved it. For some strange reason, it started at 10.10am and not 10am, and ran until 12.30pm when Dickie Davies appeared with *World of Sport*. The last hour was an episode of *Tarzan*, preceded by Tomlinson swinging across the set on a vine dressed as the jungle character and shouting, "Aargh!".

Tiswas was famous for its custard pies and buckets of water thrown at guests, including plenty of children who were housed in a large cage at the back of the studio. The Phantom Flan Flinger made regular appearances. Contestants were dragged up by their ears from under the presenters' desks. I'm sure there would be a law against it now.

In 1976, *Tiswas* got some competition when Noel Edmonds launched his *Multi-Coloured Swap Shop* on BBC1, starting at 9.30am and running for three hours until Frank Bough and *Grandstand*. The *Swap Shop* was an odd type of programme, based around the idea of swapping a toy or game at a specific location hosted by Keith Chegwin. It made stars of Cheggers, Maggie Philbin and the sweater-wearing John Craven who co-hosted in the studio with the ultra-professional and always cool Noel. There were celebrity guests and pop bands and phone-ins. I was soon converted to the *Swap Shop* though I felt a bit guilty abandoning *Tiswas*. I've just looked up the dates of these shows; both ran until 1982 though *Tiswas* outlasted *Swap Shop* by just a month. A sad loss, both of them.

The television set must have been getting warm as it was on for just about the whole of Saturday. The afternoon was devoted to sport and the rival contenders were *Grandstand* and *World of* Sport. The former was a peculiar mix of mainly live sport but cut into fifteen or twenty-minute bite-size chunks. You would get a horse race from Kempton Park followed by a burst of table tennis, then another race followed by some cricket. The idea of broadcasting a match from start to finish hadn't really occurred to anyone, except for the FA Cup Final which was always covered in depth on both channels. I became a bit obsessed with *Grandstand* and started to present my own programmes from a small table positioned near our television set. I would devise my own content, update my imaginary viewers on the football scores, and ensure I finished on the dot, ready for the next programme which might have been *The Shari Lewis And Lambchop Ventriloquist Show* or suchlike.

Over on ITV was the gloriously camp *World of Sport*. If ever a programme couldn't live up to its title, it was this one. Presented by the suave Dickie Davies - who moonlighted as a model for *Grattan's Catalogue* - the programme came live from a studio full of people furiously typing. Behind Dickie, there were rows of females maniacally tapping out reams of paper. Goodness knows what they were doing, but they were still typing when Dickie was delivering his closing remarks at five o'clock. I didn't watch *World of Sport* much, preferring the more establishment BBC fare, but it certainly had its own character.

My grandparents were fascinated by the wrestling which came on at 4pm, with Kent Walton commentating in all seriousness at what was nothing much more than an outrageous pantomime. Sandwiched into the schedules were so-called 'international sports specials'. These were often grainy tape of somewhat unusual competitions such as high diving (from cliffs, not from diving boards), billiards, power boat racing and even, on one occasion, a game of cards. Looking back, a lot of this content was probably more entertaining than *Grandstand* which took itself very seriously, but ITV was frowned upon a little in our house.

Early evening on Saturdays was dominated by *The Generation Game*, originally presented by Bruce Forsyth and then taken over by Larry Grayson. This was the era of massive audiences, there being so little choice for viewers, so some of these light entertainment offerings would attract more than ten million viewers. Bruce was the ultimate professional and such a natural, relaxed host on camera. He was able to have a laugh with contestants but never made them feel small. I loved the catchphrases; Bruce had 'Didn't he do well?' whilst Larry's was 'What a lot you've got! You have got a lot!'

After a dose of, perhaps, *Doctor Who* - my favourite always being Jon Pertwee - it was time for a variety show. The Saturday night slot was occupied by only the very best - *The Two Ronnies*, Dick Emery, Les Dawson and Mike Yarwood. I think I probably looked forward to Yarwood's programmes more than any other. He was in his heyday during the premierships of Harold Wilson, Ted Heath and Jim Callaghan but saw his star fade from 1979 when Margaret Thatcher was elected. Yarwood's impressions were pretty good and technological advances meant he was able to impersonate six people at once in some very complicated sketches. Unfortunately, when I saw him live on stage in a seaside show at Scarborough, his act was a bit stilted and the crowd seemed more into one of his support acts - The Brotherhood of Man, famous for their Eurovision winning song *Save Your Kisses For Me*.

The highlight of Saturday evenings on telly was the American import which aired around 9pm. From 1976, we were treated to *Starsky and Hutch*, the light-hearted all-action cop series starring Paul Michael Glaser and David Soul. Up until then, police shows were pretty dour with such British offerings as *Z-Cars, Dixon of Dock Green* and *Softly Softly*. Suddenly, catching criminals was exciting. Cars sped and swerved round corners, bad guys were chased over rooftops and the detectives wore snazzy clothes. *Starsky and Hutch* was fun and addictive, and I was soon acting out the shows with my childhood best mate, Gary. He was Starsky, I was Hutch and our bicycles stood in for the red and white Ford Gran Turino which featured in the real series. David Soul's sideline was music and his hit singles of the seventies, especially *Silver Lady* and *Don't Give Up On Us, Baby* captured the mood of the decade for me and I still listen to them today.

The other American imports which occupied this Saturday slot included *Cannon*, the waistband-challenged private detective, the first to have a phone in his car; *Harry O* with David Janssen, *The Rockford Files* starring James Garner and *Petrocelli*, a legal series with Barry Newman. They all presented a thrilling slice of life, much more colourful and faster-paced than 1970s Britain and we should be thankful to the BBC for exposing us to a wider worldview and a different way of living.

I don't remember much about Sundays on television. Maybe there wasn't much of it in the 1970s. However, the teatime slot was always a golden time, occupied on the BBC by a 30-minute serial such as a Dickens dramatisation starring actors such as Arthur Lowe. I can recall their version of *David Copperfield* along with other children's book adaptations like E. Nesbit's *The Phoenix From The Ashes* or *Pollyanna*.

What a wonderful way to introduce children to these great stories and I always looked forward to teatime watching one of these programmes.

In the week, the main time for telly viewing was teatime. Mother would bring in a plate of sandwiches for me. On Mondays, it might be cold roast beef. I would sit eating them whilst watching my favourite programmes. Twice a week, it was *Blue Peter* with the classic presenting trio of Valerie Singleton, Peter Purves and John Noakes, accompanied by their respective pets, Petra and Shep. Val left the show in 1972 to be replaced by Lesely Judd. I loved the programme, always broadcast live and with plenty of on-air gaffes as one might expect. The pre-Christmas show, which ended with a Salvation Army band marching in to play carols, somehow heralded the real beginning of the festive season. I once met Peter Purves, many years after his *Blue Peter* days, and he was still cracking jokes about "one I made earlier".

However, it was the daredevil Noakes who seemed to be everyone's favourite. He'd leap out of aeroplanes or climb Nelson's Column, often, we later learned, on poor wages and little insurance. My friends were split into two camps - the *Blue Peter* loyalists and the slightly audacious fans of *Magpie*, ITV's rival magazine show presented by Douglas Rae, Susan Stranks and Mick Robertson. There was something a bit bohemian and daring about *Magpie* against the Enid Blyton-esque slightly preaching manner of *Blue Peter* - and Robertson had the nerve to sport long hair as well, drawing stinging criticism from my parents. *Magpie* ran until 1980 whilst *Blue Peter* struggled on under a variety of guises. I think it's rather a shame that programmes like this don't exist anymore in the mainstream. They were fun, educational and a real talking point amongst schoolchildren.

Another ITV favourite of mine was *How!* I can still remember the line-up of presenters without looking it up - Fred Dinenage (apparently the inspiration for Alan Partridge), Jack Hargreaves, Johnny Miller and Bunty James. The format was simple: a question was posed beginning with the word *How!* Then the panel went on to answer it. Many of the questions were science or nature-based and the programme genuinely offered high-quality teaching in an accessible format. The show ran throughout the 1970s, only ending when Southern TV lost its franchise. A simple but great idea.

There are too many other gems to discuss in detail, not least the lunchtime programming which I only saw when I was off school with a cold or something, featuring *Rainbow* with Geoffrey, Bungle (a man in a bear suit) and Zippy (a puppet with a zip for a mouth), a concept so bizarre one cannot imagine it ever getting made today.

But just think of those heroes of 1970s children's television and the skill they had in leading us on, encouraging us to create, to think and to imagine: Johnny Morris, Tony Hart, Brian Cant, Floella Benjamin, Bernard Cribbins, Kenneth Williams, the *Crackerjack* team, Tony Soper, Roy Castle, Michael Rodd. The list goes on.

All I can say is thank you for the memories, thank you for the inspiration and thank you for being there for me in such a golden time.

John Howes

October 16

Milania

"I remember when we first walked into this cafe. It was late October 2015. Remember - after that crushingly boring meeting about...?" Peter hesitated, temporarily distracted by the arrival of two steaming hot lattes at their table. He gave Joana, the owner of the tiny café on Brussels' Rue de la Paix, a smile of gratitude. He remembered it well and knew the date exactly, but he was trying to melt the chilly atmosphere at their small table in the window on that damp Monday morning.

Milania picked the croissant crumbs from her plate with a moistened finger and placed them on her tongue. A sure sign that she was agitated, he knew that. She occasionally looked at Peter but seemed more interested in what was going on outside, staring through the steamed-up window.

They had made a fantastic couple at first. He: the dashing English ex-soldier, posted to the EU for five years. She: the tall, beautiful Slovakian translator, diligently translating the meetings and emailing the minutes to everyone within hours. Their affair lasted for four years and could have persisted, had he not returned to London at the end of 2019.

In the beginning, their relationship held. Monthly weekends together in Brussels or London had added an extra layer of excitement, at first. With time, the monthly trips became bi-monthly, then just occasionally. Their time together had become routine, with ever more cursory lovemaking by night and days spent eating and drinking in their old haunts, trying to find a reason for being together.

Milania finally looked at her watch, exclaiming that she was late for a meeting. They both stood up and hugged each other with genuine warmth, reminiscent of the good times. He followed her out of the café and watched her walking away. He stepped back inside the café and returned to their table. He placed two fingers to his lips and gently touched the lipstick marks on the rim of her coffee cup.

"Goodbye, my love", he whispered to himself, then stood up slowly and left.

Simon Parker

October 17

LVAR Syndrome

FaceCog's CEO, Sir Roger Thompson, stood up, stretched and went to the window to enjoy his office's million-pounds' worth of view as the morning light glinted on the buildings of Canary Wharf. As he did, someone knocked on his office door. Roger turned, went back to his desk and said, "Come in." A woman entered. Roger carefully studied her. Less than average height, slightly over-weight, dark short hair with grey flecks, wide mouth, short nose, brown eyes. It was no good. No matter how hard he tried, he couldn't recognise her.

Finally he tapped the FaceCog on his temple. The quiet reassuring voice in his tiny gold earclip said, "Susan Lewis, Head of IT."

Of course. He leaned casually back and nodded at her.

"Susan. What can I do for you?"

"It's the social media, USB and internet spyware. A guy in the research department has accessed," she glanced at the papers she held, "WhatsApp, Instagram, a betting website and a sports website over 500 times last week. Plus 700 messages via his private email, some with suspiciously large attachments."

"Bloody hell! Stealing IP?" Roger exclaimed.

"Possibly. I don't like doing this, but I need authorisation for immediate termination of employment."

She held out a form.

"Of course. We can't risk it. Get the cheating layabout out as soon as possible. And check those emails for IP leaks."

"Will do." She nodded, and left.

Bright woman, Roger thought. He quickly checked the company's share price. £781, gone up slightly. He breathed out. If that researcher had sold information to a competitor, Roger's 2,500 shares would become just so much wallpaper. He relaxed and returned to slogging through the recent emails.

+ +

Susan caught the underground to Goodge Street, her briefcase with tools, cables, spare batteries and hard-drives slung over her shoulder. Although as Head of IT she could, if she wanted, spend all her time with meetings, reports and emails, she had insisted that she stayed involved in the work at the 'coalface' – spending half a day a week helping technicians replace forgotten passwords, ensuring networks were running smoothly, monitoring the database contents, even upgrading laptops at times. How else could she ensure that the company's vital IT infrastructure was good enough?

At Montague street she pressed the intercom on the door of Roger's elegant, four-storey Georgian house.

"Yep?"

"Hi Marianne, it's Susan from work. IT stuff – again."

"Oh, sure, come in."

Marianne, Roger's wife, met her in the hall and took her coat.

"Sorry about this," Susan said. "Roger's gone and locked his account again. I need to log out his email account from his home laptop, so that I can reset it."

"Yeah, sure, it's in his office. Want a coffee?"

"Yeah, thanks. Can I have one in about half an hour? It might take me that long to sort this mess out."

Susan sat at Roger's desk and flipped open his laptop. She'd nearly done when Marianne came in with coffee and a plate of florentines.

"Do have one," she said. "I'm trying a new recipe. Dried cranberries and goji berries, chocolate infused with orange oil."

Susan took a gulp of coffee and then a florentine. "Perfect," she said. Marianne leaned back against the door frame.

"Phew!" she said breathlessly. "Fourth attempt, you know. I've spent the whole day on them, but I think I've nailed it."

"I think you have. There. Done." Susan closed the laptop and picked up her briefcase. "Back to the office, then," she said.

"OK. Ta! Roger's lucky to have you on his case. I'll get your coat."

Maybe not so lucky, Susan thought. As she put her coat on, Marianne passed her a sandwich box.

"More florentines. For the IT guys," she said. Susan muttered thanks, and left quickly. It would be a pity. Marianne was a decent person. But she and her cookery business would survive.

+   +

At last Roger had finished dealing with the urgent and important emails, as the late afternoon light faded outside. As he leaned back in his chair, his phone pinged with a message from an unknown number.

Hi, honey. I'm borrowing a friend's phone as mine is out of battery, oops! She suggested the Ottoman for our WA tonite. I've booked. Meet you there, 7pm!

Hmm. Change of venue and an earlier time? He'd not have time to go home, but he could use the manager's bathrooms to freshen up. Luckily he had Marianne's wedding anniversary gift, a voucher for spa weekend, in his desk, and the Ottoman was within walking distance.

By five past seven Roger was sitting at the table in the Ottoman, under dozens of bright stained-glass lamps that glittered and swung from the ceiling, studying the extensive and surprisingly expensive menu. A woman came in and sat opposite him in a swirl of scent, blonde hair and silk skirts. She leaned over and pecked his cheek.

"Hello, darling! Isn't this nice? Happy anniversary! Shall we have champers? Celebrate our seven years. Who says third marriages don't last?" she said in a breathless rush.

Roger recognised her scent, her cream silk Dior dress, but not her face or her voice. He tapped his FaceCog. "Marianne Thompson. Your wife," the calm voice whispered. The tiny pang of regret and guilt grabbed his throat again. He couldn't even recognise his own wife! Like hundreds of thousands of others…

"I produced perfect florentines today!" she said. They looked at the menu and had a long discussion over whether to have a starter. The champagne came and Marianne drained her glass at one go, then glanced at her watch. She seemed on edge.

Roger's phone pinged and he took it out of his pocket. Just a routine alert from work. Marianne took a plastic phone cage from her handbag and put it on the table.

"No interruptions, honey," she said. "Switch sound off, please?"

He did so. She smiled and took his phone. As she did so, she knocked the phone cage and it flew sideways.

"Oh, get that for me," she said. Roger bent to retrieve it from under the next table. Marianne had taken her phone from her bag, and deftly put both phones in the cage and twirled the padlock.

"Good boy," she winked, and kissed him. "Now, as your reward, I'm slipping to the bathroom to remove an item of clothing. See if you can guess what." The look she gave him was so saucy and lascivious that Roger couldn't help laughing as she walked to the toilets, her handbag in her hand, her skirt swishing.

The restaurant was getting busy. Roger drank another glass of champagne as he waited. Marianne seemed to be taking a while. A couple of other women had gone to the back, a woman in a cream dress but with short, curly red hair had come out but she'd left the restaurant. The waiter came up. Roger ordered the hot meze followed by iskender and sarma beyti, more champagne and waited.

+   +

Half an hour later, Roger had to accept that his wife had gone. A waitress confirmed that there was no-one in the ladies' toilet. Where the hell had Marianne gone to – what was she playing at? Some sort of off-beat wedding anniversary trick?

Roger grabbed the phone cage and wrenched apart the cheap plastic. But his phone... The unlock pattern didn't work. It wouldn't accept his code either. In fact, when he looked more closely, was it even his phone? The tiny crack on the glass protector wasn't there. He grabbed Marianne's phone and stared at it. The pale-green case looked superficially identical, but again, on close examination, it wasn't as worn as hers was.

He'd been conned! He thumped the table angrily. The nearby diners jumped. But how had he been tricked? FaceCog had told him it was Marianne and he'd stake his fortune on its reliability. They had seven of the brightest security experts and computer programmers working forty-hour weeks trying to find weaknesses and break into their databases. It couldn't possibly be hacked. So it must have been Marianne. But why?

Rapidly he paid the bill, finished the champagne and grabbed a taxi home. In the hall a woman – Marianne, he had to assume – was waiting, in a furious mood.

"You utter bastard, Roger," she yelled. "Where've you been? Drinking? I've been waiting an hour for you, you sod! On our wedding anniversary too! How could you?"

Roger stared at her, then snarled, "Sure? You little liar... Why'd you walk off? And where's my phone?"

"What? I haven't got your phone. What do you mean, walk off? I've been sitting here, waiting for my lying, two-faced husband to show up for our date, messaging you, trying to call you..."

She sounded like she was telling the truth, Roger realised.

"Shut up! Just shut up for a moment, Marianne, and listen!" he snapped. "We've been... We've been done over. Conned. Phone the police. Now! I need to change my password before that woman gets into my accounts and my email. Oh God, this could be the worst..."

Marianne's face blanched. "Roger?" she said. "Conned?"

He ignored her and dashed to his study, as she stared at him, then yanked her phone – her real phone – out of her bag. He heard her calling the police as he flipped open his home laptop.

His password didn't work. He couldn't log in. A cold dread filled him. Someone – a woman – had pretended to be Marianne and swiped his phone somehow. Probably switched phones as he bent to get the phone cage. Then walked off with his unlocked phone. And – somehow – managed to hack into his business account too. He swore. She'd be able to get at everything – his bank accounts, his emails, his secrets. He put his head in his hands and shuddered. When the police came he tried to, as calmly as he could, tell them what had happened. He was trembling. Marianne rubbed his shoulder's soothingly.

"Don't worry, Roger. It's only a phone," she said.

He shrugged. How could he tell her that it might be everything?

"Can you describe this woman?" the policeman said. "Could you recognise her again?"

Roger shook his head. "She looked like my wife," he muttered.

"Roger's got LVAR syndrome," Marianne said. "So of course he can't!"

"Of course, ma'am. Yeah, I should have remembered," the policeman said. Roger knew what he was thinking: yeah, got Lost Visual and Audio Recognition syndrome – and serves him right.

   +   +

Susan got to the office at seven. She felt exhausted. She and her daughter had spent a nerve-wracking, draining but very successful night. As she sat at her desk and waited, she checked the emails. Good. The one to all employees, telling them about the £5,000 bonus to be paid immediately, had arrived. So that had worked too.

At ten past seven the expected phone call from Roger came. He sounded desperate. In his office, Susan found him pacing the room, looking haggard and tugging at his hair so hard that strands came out in his hands. She noticed him tapping his FaceCog and pausing.

"Susan, you've got to help me," he said. "I've been hacked... Everything..."

"Not just you," she said. "FaceCog too. Look."

She tossed the newspapers onto his desk. *FaceCog databases hacked, huge data breach, LVAR syndrome sufferers 'confused and fearful', Sir Roger Thompson 'knew about LVAR syndrome years earlier'* the headlines screamed.

Roger collapsed into his chair and stared at the papers.

"Oh my God," he muttered. "How?"

"No idea," Susan lied. "But the FaceCog breach is clever."

"Clever?"

"Oh, it's neat. Only anyone with a title or MP is affected. So, Sir James Mogg-Rees truly thinks his nanny is his mother."

Roger stared at her, utter bewilderment mixing with the despair in his expression. She added salt to the wound.

"Your emails are leaked too. They show that you knew about the memory issues for ages, but suppressed it. The media is having a wonderful day with all this."

His shoulders slumped even more. Suddenly he laid his head down on the desk. "That's it, then," he muttered.

Susan ignored the twinge of pity. Her husband had been a respected head of the Maths department in a private school but after getting LVAR syndrome he had had to leave. Not even FaceCog could be fast enough for a teacher to recognise and deal with thirty children. Although now her husband managed to do online tutoring, he was broken, like so many others. Almost as broken as Roger was now. But Roger didn't have a beloved spouse who clutched his temples, crying, "I know I have a wife and daughter, friends, but I don't know what they look like! What they sound like!" Who looked emptily at their red-haired actress daughter, who stared at Susan with utter blankness, until that vile FaceCog butted in with its muttered, "Susan, your wife" and she saw the puzzled look fade into a bitter, painful smile.

Susan turned on her heel and left.

  +   +

As the door slammed, Roger looked up. Silently he cursed himself. He should never have got involved with that memory-enhancing drug. But, free from the EU red tape and restrictions, selling and investing it had been an irresistible gold mine. It turned out that thousands – millions – of people wanted a better memory. And he should have listened to, not suppressed, the reports of infrequent but odd side-effects: confusion, loss of the ability to remember and recognise faces and voices. Instead – what a fool! – he'd carried on taking it himself. He'd needed a sharp mind and accurate memory. God, he'd made a fortune until the truth came out. And a second fortune joining together with a bright AI entrepreneur to start FaceCog.

Well, it was all gone now. Ruin and desolation, and it was his own fault. There was nothing left he could do. No point in trying to trace the leak, find out who'd conned him, or how it had been done. He was finished. Game over. He walked to the window and opened it wide.

Cathy Hemsley

October 18

Village Memories

I had a lovely thank you card popped through my letterbox for being friendly from Karen who used to live up by Edgar Robinson. I remembered her but thought she lived nearer me. Never mind - I had remembered her.

Her partner had owned a big black bike and black leathers and horn-rimmed glasses. I think he was Mike. They were very young. I think she worked in a nursery.

Today, I went down to the church hall for a butty and a coffee. There was a lovely lot of people there. I can only attend at holiday time when I am not doing German at the Guildhouse. I could talk to my neighbour, Sylvia, and help her with her mug and her tea. Sylvia is well into her eighties and on her own now. She has a good family, though it is still lonely. We reminisced and I told her about our waitressing in the local pub on a Saturday night. I remembered that Karen used to come down and help me at the playgroup. She was nice and gentle with the children; she also spent quite a lot of time in our house drinking tea and sympathy. It was so nice to meet up and see the confident young woman she has become. She thanked me for making her welcome and introducing her to folks.

I moved over to the other side of the room to sit next to Gwyneth. She is now over ninety and her son Stephen lives at home with her. He looks after her and no doubt she thinks she looks after him. I did not get time to chat with Pauline today. She was probably peeved but she is pretty good at getting attention for herself! Sylvia was complaining how the village is changing. We used to have a shop and there would be a card on the counter saying if someone was ill or in hospital, or who had a baby and a tin collection box. There is a village Facebook page but older people do not know how to use it. I still like my village very much.

Ruth Hughes

October 19

Peregrine Lockdown

After two weeks of lockdown, I'd started contemplating divorce from my once-wonderful husband, and then in the third week he snapped back into being his considerate self. True, he didn't bring me weekly flowers as he'd been doing for the last eighteen months or so. Difficult to get, I suppose. I haven't seen any in the shops round here lately and then he came back from a jog with a bunch of daffs.

'I picked them through the park railings. Locked. No one around to see.'

He's a risk-taker is my Alex.

Our lockdown was going to be a good one, it seemed. Better than my neighbour with no family who lived alone. 'It's all this media stuff about folk missing their family. Gets me down at times,' she'd moan. And we were certainly more harmonious than the couple whose wine-fuelled rows were the entertainment/bugbear of our tiny close.

This new jogging hobby was making him affable. Working from home was no problem for him, an academic at our local university. Sitting alone at his computer undistracted was his preferred method of work and he approached it with total seriousness.

But he was finding more time for our daughter, too. If she sat at her lap-top keeping me company in the kitchen, he would join her when he emerged downstairs for a coffee.

'That's one of our peregrines back, then. The bio lab boys must have put the web-cam up again.' He'd come up behind her and was looking over her shoulder.

And he would stop and watch for peregrines with her, though not consistently. He could soon get restless, whip on his jogging suit and go off out.

I suppose there's only so much he could take of watching a bird sitting on an egg, or not.

'Let's check out our peregrine,' he'd say if she wasn't logged in to it but he could soon be off out. My daughter had more patience. She didn't need her dad's company to watch. In time she was watching three flightless chicks of the swiftest bird in the world in their lofty lockdown. At times a parent would bring newly-caught prey, usually a pigeon, and she'd watch it being dismembered and fed to the competing chicks.

I couldn't watch it too long with her. Too gruesome for me. And too like my preparation of chicken breasts for our meals.

My husband was becoming keen on keeping fit. No red meat; low fat and low salt was on his menu now and I'd patiently traipse around to stand spaced apart in one supermarket queue after another.

'Dad's low salt thingee's working' said my daughter once, after her dad had rapidly disappeared upstairs for a post-jog shower. Helping Mum was the game and she'd gathered up his sweaty navy track-suit. 'Look, no white salty marks.' Amazing what a nine-year old notices. They notice more than us though they understand less, I hope.

Feathers, flies and bones were accumulating on the birds' pebbly nesting tray. The two parent birds, both efficient slaughtering machines, kept up their supply of still warm prey. A demanding task, for one nestling appeared to be weakening. Then it disappeared. Fed to its siblings. 'Practical,' was her comment. 'They're not being cruel.'

Once she'd seen a bright yellow triangle on the ledge. 'What's that? Oh yuk, I think one of them must've brought back a blackbird.'

My husband ignored her, whipped on his track-suit and dashed off.

'Well, I'd have stayed to check that out.' I felt indignant at his restlessness and abrupt dismissal of his daughter.

'Oh no, he always goes out if the window in the corner has a light in it. The one you can see in the distance. Down on the street. It's on dad's run.'

I continued ironing. And about ten minutes later heard, 'Ah, there goes dad.'

The next time he jogged off I joined her at her screen. Beyond the birds' nesting ledge, you could see a bit of the ground further away, down to the street that had the Old People's Home round its corner and now had, ominously, two ambulances going along it. 'There goes dad,' I heard and I saw him jog on the spot waiting for them to pass, so he could cut along the lane that leads to a rough grassy space if you follow the high wall on the right; saw him take that route by the wall to jog past the red gate in it; saw him turn and jog in through that gate. The gate that opens into the old house where some of the young office staff live and one window was lit. A light went out.

He returned within his permitted hour and disappeared swiftly upstairs. I picked up his still damp running shell. No salt marks. I smelt it. No more smell than if it'd been dampened by... tap water. When he reappears he'll step down humming, all affable, Mr OnceWonderful.

To risk his health, his life, my life. Our daughter's life. For a roll in the hay? No not even that – more like the thrill of risk. It enhanced the sex. The peregrine that fed its own dead chick to its siblings was not frivolous or selfish. I'll show him risk, all right. He'll live with risk now.

Well, what do you do in a lockdown? The normal reactions are limited and do not apply and I have the rest of lockdown to think. He's deceiving me, he'll think, but he'll be the deceived one.

My immediate thought was a yew-berry curry but I reckon I can improve on that. I'll be as efficient as a peregrine.

Chris Rowe

October 20

Marrying Elvis

I was not one of those children who knew exactly what they were going to do when they grew up. I was envious of my school friends who knew, by the age of ten, that they would be doctors, chiropodists or hairdressers. The first career I can remember aspiring to was that of a bus conductor. I would spend hours arranging my toys on the stairs, moving gingerly between them, shaking loose coins borrowed from our money jar in one of mum's brown leather handbags. I would issue my passengers with authentic yellow bus tickets from rolls given to me by our kindly local bus driver.

After that, my career plans became vague. I dallied with the idea of being an air hostess but lost interest when the British Airways recruitment leaflet informed me I was too short. I considered being an Olympic athlete but realised this might not be possible when I got beaten by my best friend in the discus at our school sports day.

But, at the age of 12, there was one thing of which I was completely certain. I knew that I was going to marry Elvis.

From the time I purchased my first 45 vinyl record which was Elvis singing *Crying in the Chapel,* and after I saw him in the film *Blue Hawaii*, I knew there would never be anyone else for me. There was the slight issue of geography to overcome. He was unlikely to meet me in the small Scottish town where I lived, especially as he had a fear of flying. It would be difficult for me to get over to meet him, but I knew that once I did, our fates would be sealed.

I was a member of the British Elvis Presley fan club and one day, I read an advertisement in their magazine. A weeklong trip to Memphis to see where Elvis lived and worked, culminating in top seats at one of his live concerts. This was my chance. I knew that if I could get in front of him and our eyes could meet, my work would be done, and we would spend the rest of our days together.

The price of this life changing opportunity was £215 but with only 20p a week pocket money, I soon worked out that it might take too long to get to America and my chance of happiness would be lost. I worked out a new plan. I stopped going to the sweet shop each week and saved my pennies instead. I negotiated an increase of 5p per week pocket money in return for ironing my dad's thick RAF blue cotton shirts. I asked mum to cancel my *Jackie* magazine subscription which she collected each week with her *People's Friend*. Mum and Dad agreed to let me have the money for the magazine, provided I opened a high interest savings account at the post office. Dad explained to me that the interest I would earn on the money would add to my own and help accelerate the time taken to reach my goal of £215.

I remember how proud my dad was on the day we walked up to the post office to open my non-easy access high interest savings account. The lady behind the counter seemed quite bemused by my eagerness to save.

'What are you saving up for?' she asked me over the top of her dark rimmed glasses.

'I'm going to marry Elvis,' I replied.

The look that was exchanged between herself and my dad did not go unnoticed, and, for just a few seconds, I wondered if she, too, wanted to marry Elvis.

She finished preparing the book and paperwork and I had to sign a couple of bits of paper. My dad countersigned. Finally she asked me for my deposit. I reluctantly handed over the contents of my piggy bank, just under £3. She took the money, counted it out carefully before slotting it into the coin storage by her side. She placed my open book into her machine and I could hear it typing something. She took it back out, checked it and then passed it out to me through her silver drawer.

I walked home with my dad, proudly clutching my first savings account book. It was a very smart silver-covered paying in book and on the first line of the first page it had my opening balance of £2.72. I was on my way to Memphis.

+   +

Over the next few months, I focussed relentlessly on reaching my goal of £215. I did as many extra chores at home as my parents would allow. I abstained from all sweets and crisps, and I started my first (and only) financial scam with my grandfather.

I was an avid nail biter. I had tried everything to stop, including the horrid tasting polish that you painted on. I soon became used to its bitter taste as I happily chewed away at my nails. My grandfather detested girls with chewed nails and, on one visit, knowing I was saving up, offered me 15p per nail if I stopped biting them and could show him 10 pristine nails on his next visit.

And much to everyone's surprise, I stopped biting my nails. The chance of moving £1.50 closer to my goal was more irresistible than the comforting taste of crunchy nails and soft skin.

On his next visit, I proudly revealed my hands with their newly formed nails, somewhat squint but complete with visible white bits on the top. After inspection, he presented me with £1.50.

That evening, after my grandparents departed, I set about, with quiet satisfaction, chewing at my newly formed nails. I managed to get another two lots of £1.50 out of my grandfather before he realised he was on a hiding to nothing.

Greatly helped by my grandfather's nail payments, I felt I was well on the way to my target. I would make weekly trips to the post office, averting my eyes from all the chocolate, crisps and magazines as I headed to the payment kiosk at the back of the shop. Often it was the same lady with the dark-rimmed glasses who was behind the counter and even though she always smiled when she handed my book back to me, I remained suspicious of her intentions towards Elvis.

I had just turned 13 and was more focused than ever on marrying Elvis when something utterly dreadful and life changing happened. Elvis died. He died. Alone in his bathroom, on the toilet. He died never realising that I would soon be on my way to make him happy.

After Elvis died, everything changed. What was the point of anything now, let alone saving for a trip that would now never happen?

I had £15.84 in my little silver book and no purpose in life.

'I want to close my savings account. There's no point in saving anymore now that Elvis is dead,' I announced to my dad shortly after that dreadful day.

'There's always a point to saving, Hen,' he replied. 'They'll be someone else for you. You'll soon find another Elvis.'

'There will never be another Elvis. Not for me. Not ever.'

Begrudgingly my dad walked me back up to the post office. All the way there he begged me to re-think and not close the account. He was a shrewd Scotsman who had never had much money and he was so keen for me to save wisely for the life to come. I rarely remember him being as animated as he was on that day.

'Please don't close the account, Hen. You've done so well. What if I match what you save this month? Penny for penny. You'll find something you want to save again for soon.'

My mind was made up. I handed over my little silver book to the lady behind the counter and, in return, took my £15.84. I headed to Boots the Chemist and spent the next hour mulling over what to spend my riches on.

I settled for some Rimmel make-up and a whole selection of sandalwood bath products. I bought a large presentation box. There was a bright orange flannel, a lovely tin of talcum powder, some small translucent balls of bubble bath and some cubes of bath salts that stay gritty and scratchy on the base of the bath long after they should have dissolved.

I still love the smell of sandalwood but it always makes me think of Elvis dying. And whilst I can no longer cling onto that wonderful childhood naivety that was taking me to Memphis, I still believe that had our eyes met during that concert, we really would have fallen in love and I would have married Elvis.

Fiona White

October 21

One Last Time

When the phone rang that evening, I knew it would be my mother. I guessed what was wrong. No need to ask.

I threw a few essentials into my backpack and phoned for a taxi.

The train was on time. Crowded. Hot. I tried to read.

Another taxi, then I was walking up the path.

The smell of rotting vegetation was heavy in the air.

As I reached for the bell, my mother opened the door.

"How is he?" I asked.

"He's gone," she said, as if he had just left for work, or the pub, or to take the dog for a run.

Matter of fact. Dry. No tears.

"It hasn't sunk in," I thought.

I did not hug her. Just the usual peck on the cheek.

Emotion is not my line. I could not force it.

Not after all I had gone through for years while she slept.

Her eyes pierced mine. No tears. No emotion.

So that was it.

She knew.

Wendy Goulstone

October 22

Ferdinand

Colin the Manager carried Ferdinand's poor body back to the hotel after his ordeal. His service had been exemplary, so the eccentric escape was even more baffling.

Unlike the other staff, Colin the Manager felt inexplicable grief over Ferdinand's loss and arrangements for his replacement would have to be made.

But why the break for freedom? All the other cleaners were happy in their servitude. Just look at the floor, thought Colin. Yet Ferdy went straight out the front door at top speed surprising everyone and was half a mile away before anyone could react. Only clumsiness and a ditch, and a hedge and the Cambridge frost could stop Ferdinand.

People speculated as to what had happened in his tiny mind. Was it a natural consequence of all of that menial work or a flare up of individual spirit to blaze and die like a shooting star?

Colin sighed and prepared the funeral in the light electricals recycle bin. The only mystery left was why the other cleaning robots didn't throw a gasket, take off down the Newmarket Road to the countryside and end up broken.

Colin snapped out of his romantic daze. Pragmatically, he salvaged Ferdinand's battery for the others, Lineker, Rooney, Shearer and the rest. It would be easy enough to order a few more from PC World.

A name? Kane? Owen? Yes... Stirling!

Chris Wright

October 23

Nightmare On Elf Street

The storm was right overhead. Lightning streaked across the sky, closely followed by the crash of angry thunder. Rain lashed against Rapunzel's tower and her hair, caught by the wind, was tangled up in the gutter. Her shrieks of pain as her heavy plaits were tugged yet again were lost in the howling wind and the rumble of thunder.

The heavy gusts blew away all three of the Little Pigs' houses. The Big Bad Wolf was delighted as he hunted the squealing piglets through the woods and caught them one by one. Mrs. Big Bad and their cubs, warm and safe in their den in a cosy, snug cave halfway up the mountain, would be eating well for the next few days.

The Gingerbread Witch wasn't faring so well as her Gingerbread Cottage had dissolved in the rain. Hansel and Gretel ran off, giggling. She was wet, homeless and hungry, but she managed to save some of her possessions before the wind whisked them away. Wrapping her bedraggled cloak around herself, she trudged off in search of somewhere to stay. Maybe her sister, Rapunzel's witch, would put her up.

A savage bolt of lightning speared Snow White's glass coffin, showering the forest with pieces of glass. One large shard pierced her Prince's heart and he collapsed at her feet. The Seven Dwarves came running, but they were too late. The lightning strike had jolted the piece of poisoned apple from Snow White's mouth. She woke and saw the corpse of her would-be lover. The Dwarves took the hysterical princess back to their cottage. Once Snow White had calmed down, they went to check whether their diamond mine had been flooded. Perhaps someday another Prince would come.

Water gushed through the Three Bears' cottage. They watched glumly as their chairs, beds and porridge bowls floated off. Luckily Goldilocks was asleep on one of the beds (the smallest one, belonging to

Baby Bear), so at least they didn't have to worry about feeding the great, greedy lump in the morning.

Red Riding Hood's Grandma was in dire trouble. The Wicked Wolf had arrived and gobbled her up. He was sitting up in bed, dressed in Grandma's night-dress (this was the part he enjoyed the best), her glasses perched on the end of his big nose, waiting for Red Riding Hood to arrive. However, because of the dreadful weather, Red Riding Hood's mother had refused to let her go out. And the Woodcutter had packed up early and gone home. It's not easy cutting down trees in the rain. So the Wicked Wolf waited in vain as Grandma slowly digested in his stomach. In the morning she would be gone and he would have chronic indigestion. She was a tough, stringy old biddy. He much preferred the tender, succulent flesh of youth.

Midnight chimed and Cinderella ran down the palace steps, leaving one glass slipper behind for Prince Charming. The road had turned to mud and her coach couldn't get through. Prince Charming saw what he was not supposed to see, as the dazzling beauty dressed in an exquisite ball gown turned into a dirty, scruffy scullery maid wearing rags. Disgusted he tossed her shoe away and went back into the palace. He danced the night away with Princess Floribelle from the next kingdom. The King had always wanted him to marry her and so he did. They lived happily ever after, producing a brood of dull but worthy children.

As the glass slipper shattered so did Cinderella's hopes. She arrived home cold, wet and miserable. Her Fairy Godmother was eagerly awaiting her return and asked if she had enjoyed the Ball. Something deep inside Cinderella snapped and she beat the astonished Fairy to death with her broom. Then she lay in wait for her hated step-sisters and their horrible mother. When they arrived, she hit them over the head with the flat-iron and set fire to the house. The rain prevented it from burning down, but they all died anyway, asphyxiated by the fumes from the cheap furniture Baron Hardup had bought at a car boot sale. He was happy to claim the insurance, being wildly over-insured, but Buttons was inconsolable. He had thought he would be in with a chance after Prince Charming had turned his nose up at Cinderella.

On the other side of the mountain, Princess Aurora was about to prick her finger when a loud crash of thunder made her jump and she knocked over the spinning wheel. The King burst into the room in time to save his daughter and the Wicked Fairy cursed as she was dragged off to the deepest, darkest, dankest dungeon. She should have saved her breath. Aurora did not meet her Prince and died an old maid. Her kingdom was fought over for many years, causing much bloodshed. The Prince who was supposed to be her husband was greatly relieved that she was dead before he was born because he preferred princes to princesses.

In the woods, instead of being warm and cosy beneath a blanket of leaves, the Babes were slowly freezing to death. Hansel and Gretel encountered the Big Bad Wolf, who was delighted to find another meal. His cubs were always hungry.

The Beanstalk blew down, crushing Jack's mother's cottage and killing her. Jack was trapped in the Giant's castle. He tried to hide, but the Goose who Laid the Golden Eggs gave him away. The Giant did indeed grind Jack's bones to make his bread. In fact the Giant had him toasted for breakfast, spread with a thick layer of lime marmalade. Delicious.

+   +

In the morning, the Fairy Godmother waved her wand and put everything back the way it was supposed to be.

The Wicked Fairy watched and sniggered. She had plans for later that day that would make yesterday seem like a walk in the park.

Fran Neatherway

October 24

If Only

He stood immobile, back-lit in the open-curtained bay window of the first floor flat, his hands shoved into the front pockets of his jeans. His eyes slowly focused on the street, beyond the rain splattered glass. The park opposite was a black nothingness, the fence lit-up occasionally by the odd passing car. The street lamp down the road seemed to illuminate nothing except a large and growing puddle. A figure hurried by, head down against the driving rain, and was gone.

Part of the darkness suddenly broke free from his neighbour's garden hedge, drifted the length of the low wall, and paused at the gateway; then flowed along the path. For a brief, fleeting, second a moonglow patch glimmered amid the shapeless black. A face. It was gone before he could register any features, but still, it stirred something... AND he turned his back to the glass, expectantly awaiting a knock on the door, or the bell to ring.

Nothing. The silence expanded. Not for him, then; not who he thought he'd seen. Imagined he'd seen? There was a click, as if a glass had suddenly cracked, such a flicker of quiet sound he wondered if he'd actually heard it. Galvanised into motion he ran for the stairs, the entrance hall, the door.

The amorphous black shape was just moving away, but stopped, turned, resolved. Head to foot in sodden black – it was her.

Nothing was said, but she stepped into the dark hallway. Taking her hand, he climbed the stairs, and led her into the warm flat. He settled her into a chair, found her a towel, and then retreated to the kitchen to make a hot drink. Bracing himself against the worksurface, he waited for his legs to stop shaking, and support him again. Why her? Why now?

This he could do without.

EE Blythe

October 25

Reg Loves That Bonsai

"Reg loves that dratted plant more than me. He's called it 'Belinda' and taken 'her' for another trim. The second time this week. There must be somebody in the garden centre that he fancies." Judy was moaning to her best friend, Gene who had called for a coffee.

"I was going for my Monday morning swim. I called as I was worried because you didn't reply to my text. Don't worry about Reg. Aren't you going for your annual Spain trip? Surely Reg wouldn't stray? You've been married for thirty happy years. It's not possible Reg would throw everything away," said Gene.

"We were visiting Spain but he's changed his mind, again. He doesn't ask what I think, he doesn't seem to care. The excuse is that he can't leave the garden! The plants need watering and there's nobody to do it. The baskets and bedding plants would die. I've heard of excuses, the cat, the dog, the mother-in-law. But plants, I ask you. I'm worried about our marriage," Judy said as she hung her head and sniffed for effect.

"Is he at the garden centre now?" asked Gene.

"Yes, Mondays he's always at the centre with Belinda the bonsai and his fancy woman. He's at Boxall's Mondays, Wednesdays and Fridays," said Judy.

"Come on then, get your coat. We can go to Boxall's now. I can swim another day."

Gene wanted to sort Reg and Judy. They'd been friends since their school days, married the same year and had their two children a few months apart, a boy and a girl. They'd helped each other through difficult times, especially when Reg lost his job and Judy was made redundant.

"We can sort Reg, together. Put your coat on, Judy. How's about a bit of lipstick and some makeup? Would you like me to do it for you?" said Gene.

"I'm not doddery, yet. I haven't lost my marbles," said an annoyed Judy.

"I didn't want to upset you," Gene said. "I'll wait in the car. I need to be home by three to let the plumber in to mend the washing machine." She couldn't bear the thought of losing Judy's friendship.

"I'm ready. There, not that slow, was I?" Judy couldn't resist the sarcasm.

"A perfect transformation. You're looking good as usual." Gene waited a few minutes as her friend locked the house, got into the passenger seat and Gene drove off.

"Destination Boxall's," she said. "Reg loves you, always has. Sometimes he has difficulty showing you how much he cares. You're lucky you share holidays, the theatre and bridge."

"We used to. Since we've retired everything has changed. Apart from gardening and that silly bonsai, he isn't interested," Judy muttered.

"Boxall's is only half an hour away. It's scenic and quicker through the village."

"Reg always takes the motorway. He never listens to me. We watch the telly and he's always falling asleep. Unless his heart-throbs Alan Titchmarch or Monty Don are on another gardening programme. Then we sit in silence. Gardening is a new passion and he suddenly likes to watch Gardener's World and glued to anything remotely garden-orientated."

Gene realised Judy was jealous of Reg and his gardening. "It's great Reg has an interest in gardening. Many retired gents just sit at the computer or watch telly. At least Reg is in the fresh air and interested in gardening."

"That's not all. I've told him loads of times that Dan is away with work. He keeps asking when you're both coming round for dinner. I give up."

"Why don't you come for dinner on Saturday?" Gene realised it would be good for their friendship to have dinner and catch up with Dan.

"It's great he's away all week. There's time to keep on top of things around the house. How's his new contract with the HS2 going?" Judy asked as they arrived at Boxall's.

Gene parked the car and they walked in the garden centre. "We'll chat about Dan and his job over dinner. Let's go for a coffee and Boxall's famous cake. What do you say, Judy?"

"Good idea. Last time the scones were dry, and crumbly. Perhaps they've improved. I don't come here in case I see Reg with his floozy! He doesn't even ask me to come with him to Boxall's."

Gene was annoyed with her grumpy friend. "Let's try different cakes. Please cheer up. I'd like my old cheery friend back. I need a good friend when Dan's away. Our time together is precious. Don't you agree, Judy? I'd like a positive Judy back. I'm sure you've nothing to worry about."

Judy had changed that much; maybe Reg's head has been turned.

"I don't like Boxall's changes, the small outlets within the store, just like all the other garden centres. I like only plants and associated garden items in garden centres. Perhaps you could share Reg's interest in the garden," suggested Gene.

Judy flushed a bright red, her eyes almost popped out of their sockets as she spluttered and attempted an answer.

"Gene, you know I hate gardening. Ever since Dad fell ill. Mum gave him aconites to eat. He was terribly allergic, ended up in hospital. I've been off plants ever since. Mum thought the yellow of the aconite flower would cheer up his salad. Dad never seemed the same again. Can you blame me hating anything to do with gardening?" shouted Judy as she stomped off towards the café. She didn't glance at anything.

Gene caught up with her friend. "Sorry, Judy. I forgot. We can't fall out today. We're here for a coffee." And she muttered under her breath that the poisoning happened fifteen years ago. Judy didn't hear.

"Reg has taken up gardening safe in the knowledge that I'll never join him in the garden or look at the flowers. I don't have a clue what they're called. He loves his plants and grows flowering plants for colour all the year round. It's breathtakingly beautiful, but I don't ever tell him that!" said Judy.

"How's his allotment? It's a lot of work, but great that he grows his own veggies."

"Yes, they're amazing, I love his vegetables. Now he forbids me to buy any in the supermarket. He grows and preserves all our veg. He's taken control of the cooking. Don't talk to me about plants, flowers or veg."

"All right, Judy, I get the message. Shame, I didn't realise how strongly you felt. Let's queue for that coffee and cake. I'm ready for it, the smell of freshly baked bread is intoxicating. I'm starving. The café's the far end right hand corner."

They walked quickly. Judy had changed dramatically over the last two years since they'd stopped working together in the office and Gene had to do something about her best friend. They'd worked on neighbouring computers for thirty years. They were like sisters, often bickering, but they enjoyed the making up, maybe visiting a tea room, coffee shop or the exquisite décor in the smart French restaurant on the other side of town. That meant serious making up. Maybe this was an occasion when Le Petit was the venue for repairing their friendship.

"Let's go straight to the Planty Coffee Shop. We need a slice of the largest, chocolatiest cake – that one in the centre of the cabinet. It looks scrummy, chocolate butter cream in the middle, choc icing on top with small flake pieces. Fancy a slice, Judy?"

"Yummy, yes please, it looks delicious." Judy actually smiled.

"Great to see you smile, Gene."

Judy sat at a table as Gene purchased the cake. She scanned around, looking for Reg and his fancy woman.

"There's Reg, it's the back of his head," Judy whispered, noticing a few grey hairs in an otherwise full head of dark brown hair, maybe more grey than usual. "Oh, he's turned around. It isn't Reg. Good job it wasn't as he's just kissed that much younger blonde lady. Reg lives another day. Gene, please bring me on Wednesday at the same time. Maybe I'll see him and I'll try to be more cheerful."

"Right, I'll take you home when we've finished this delish cake. Coffee and brownies next time, and you pay. I don't have long on Wednesday; Sally, my daughter-in-law, is bringing the grandchildren for lunch," said Gene.

The two friends walked quickly through the centre not looking at anything; Gene didn't want Judy to find Reg with another woman.

+ +

Judy was ready and waiting at ten on Wednesday. Gene noticed Judy had been to the hairdresser's and had her greying hair coloured. It suited her and she was wearing a pink flowery, cotton shirtwaist dress. She'd made an amazing effort.

"Wow. You look lovely, Judy, in the new dress you bought last week. I love your new pink hair, it suits you. We can go now, I don't have long for coffee. You looked that grumpy on Monday I didn't think I'd see the old Judy back," said Gene, giving Judy a kiss and rattling her keys as she turned to open the car door.

Judy took the hint and grabbed her red handbag from the hall table, and slid into her high- heeled red shoes, usually saved for special occasions.

"It's a red shoes day, then? I'm sure there'll be a positive result with Reg. Here we are, that was a quick journey."

"Thanks for the support, Gene. I must discover what Reg is up to. I'll order a first coffee. If you want a wander around the flowers, I'll wait for you," said Judy and walked off.

Gene looked at a few plants; she didn't want to keep her friend waiting but she didn't have time to hang around. As Gene sat down with Judy, they were amazed to see, yes, it was Reg walking their way. He seemed to see them and dodged into the card section. There was a puzzled lady walking behind Reg. She frowned as she concentrated on what Reg was saying. The lady was attractive, tall, slim with jet black, short wavy hair and much younger, only about fifty, if that.

"That's him, Gene, that's Reg. What's he doing with that lady? She has a trolley full of plants, and stuff. I'll sort him out." Judy slammed her cup onto the table and caught hold of Gene's arm as she brushed past.

"Take a deep breath. There might be a good explanation." Gene attempted to calm and reassure her friend.

"Reg, stop, Reg. I'm behind you. Caught you in the act. What are you doing with her?" Judy marched up to Reg, barring his way. She looked down. "Reg, that's a Boxall's uniform. What's going on? Why are you here? Why didn't you tell me?" said Judy.

"Don't worry, darling. I've been working here for three months. I love it but didn't think you would approve. I couldn't bear to be under your feet at home all the time and the money is handy to pay for the garden and our trips out, of course," said Reg, putting his arm around Judy.

"This explains everything. You should've told me. It's a brilliant idea. I might even take up gardening to help you," said a smiling Judy as she gave her husband a kiss on the cheek. "I'll have tea ready on the table when you get home."

When the women were in the car, Gene leant across Judy, opened the glove compartment and took out an envelope.

"Here, good friend, a present, open it," said Gene.

"How exciting. I wonder what it can be. I love surprises." Judy ripped open the gold envelope and discovered an invitation to the Le Petit restaurant.

"Great idea, Gene. We're not busy on Saturday and would love to meet up. Thanks," said Judy and hugged her best friend.

Kate A Harris

October 26

Egg And Chips

"Do you still love me?" asked Clare.

This was going to be awkward. I'd been seeing her for a couple of months. She was one of our receptionists and, after a bit of friendly banter, we'd started going out. Most lunchtimes we would meet up and wander round town together. Until this one. I'd made an excuse about work overload and decided instead to go out for egg and chips with my mate, Roger Tilsley. And very good the egg and chips were at the Shakespeare pub round the corner.

Trouble was, on the way back to the office, we ran into Clare by the pedestrian crossing. She'd spotted us a while back and came up to me in tears.

"We'll talk about it later," I mumbled. Roger kept his silence. When things stopped for tea in the afternoon, Clare and I used our usual phone signal to meet in the office kitchen. I can't remember what excuse I came up with, maybe something about discussing a project with Roger, but - deep down - the whole thing was just an example of me trying to exercise power in a relationship and my unfailing skill in self-destructing promising relationships.

So, it was no surprise that, a few weeks later, Clare and I were standing in the early chill of the car park one summer evening. I wanted to discuss the decreasing frequency of her phone calls, the decline in our office banter, and my birthday outing when she hardly said a word in front of my friends and gave me a stilted peck on the cheek to say goodbye.

After a few awkward silences, I could hardly believe it when I came up with, "Clare. Do you still love me?" Well, you can probably guess the rest.

John Howes

October 27

Why I Love Life

I do not want to die yet given a choice. I still enjoy life. Yes my spine is pretty worn out now, and I am 77, but given a choice, I would rather carry on at the moment. Logically at this age the odds are not good, but what the heck!

I once had to share a room with another actress called Dana. We were doing murder mysteries together. Dana was a depressive person who dressed always in purple and dyed her hair purple too. She smoked and snored and moaned in the night; ear plugs are not that useful! Now she did have an unwell daughter which can't have helped but she had a newish partner who did all the cooking and brought her breakfast in bed each morning. She had recovered from cancer, but she said she didn't care if she died tomorrow, a bit like the mournful robot in *The Hitchhikers' Guide to the Galaxy*. Rather her than me.

There is so much I would miss. I love life, I have family, I live in a lovely place and at the time of lockdown we had a great-grandson born. When I realised that I would be able to see him each weekend he kept me sane. He is three now and I love seeing the world through his eyes, and he seems to like me too.

Ruth Hughes

October 28

In The Pink

'Not quite as pretty as her sister was at her age, is she? Such lovely golden curls she had.'

'I'm browner, but I'm brighter,' rasped a steady voice.

The woman looked down at the deficient little girl. Her gaze was met with disturbingly direct scrutiny.

'That's such a pretty dress, such a lovely pink,' said the woman in hopes of conciliation.

'I don't like pink.' The intensity of the child's scowl made her drop her shopping bag, but she didn't give up.

'Don't be silly. All little girls like pink. It's their colour.'

'I hate pink. Silly pink. Why is your hair two colours?'

'It's not. It's brown like yours.'

'Mine hasn't got a grey stripe down the middle.'

The mother decided it was time they went. As they moved off along the pavement, a fading voice could be heard 'Can I have a grey stripe in my hair? Silly pink. Why don't boys have to wear it?'

They left the woman, as we must do, too, for she has no further place in this story, or perhaps the child retained some memory of her, but home she went with her parent to enter their modest home, where she shared a room with her big sister, who did like pink; and time moved on. And in time, too, she inhabited her elder sister's clothes, overwhelmingly pink, and sometimes, to the girl's disgust, with sparkles. One unsuccessful attempt to remove them had created so many ladders as to make the top unwearable. She grew into her sister's discarded bike, pink, of course, was forbidden to repaint it – they could perhaps even sell it when her turn came to outgrow it.

She lived a life of inherited pink. She shared a bedroom with a pink-obsessed elder sister whose taste in furnishing prevailed. They got on well together, however. The elder, while cherishing her own natural attractiveness, recognised her younger sister's cleverness. In her teenage years, the elder's light hair became even blonder, while her sister tried reading Dickens. In decisions the natural authority of the elder prevailed, but she looked after her brighter sibling. There was an eight-year gap between them and the elder felt some proprietorial interest in her, for had she not even suggested her name, Rose. One day, sighing that she wished it had been her name, she received the reply: 'You can have it if you want. It'd suit you better. I don't like being called Rose or yuk even worse, Rosie. Swap you.' Her mother pointed out the impracticalities of the scheme and it was scrapped.

In self-defence Rose learned to cultivate, mostly, an indifference to pink. She was probably the only girl to enjoy wearing her bottle-green school uniform.

Came the day her elder sister vacated the room to live with her boyfriend. Rose acquiesced in the request that she leave the room unaltered – oh how her fingers itched to remove the overbearing pinkety pinkness of it all – but, well, she conceded that her sister might return, but an engagement was announced. Wedding plans were being made; Rose was to be chief bridesmaid. Grumbling that she knew what colour she'd have to wear, she heard, 'I don't care if Sallie chooses orange with black stripes and purple circles. It's her day, her choice and you'll wear it.'

'She could wear pink herself.'

'Don't be silly – brides always wear white.'

'Want to bet? She could have a pale pink dress.'

''Well, yes, she is – but you bridesmaids are wearing cherry pink.'

'Yuk.'

Came the morning, with the usual flurry of last-minute preparations. The style of dress ordered for Rose had pleased her so much that she'd had a blue-green shorter version. Perhaps it was a bribe to render her compliant. Her suggestion that she wear it instead met with a flat refusal. But, well, she'd soon have a room all to herself, from which pink, every hint and tint of it, would be removed, abolished, eradicated! Yippee.

So near her goal – could she restrain her dissatisfaction just one day more?

Rose, in pink, chief bridesmaid, stood with the others in the tiny kitchen, waiting for the car. They'd had a quick drink to steady their nerves; rosé, of course, Rose noted, and opted for coffee instead, but it didn't deprive her of a pun – 'Here's to my sister's rosy future!' as she swept up her coffee with a flourish and her cerise bodice received a big blotch of spreading brown.

Amid the howls of anguish hers was the voice of calm authority:

'No matter. I can wear my turquoise. It's the same style, so it'll fit in. It'll look deliberate. Sallie's still upstairs in the bathroom. Don't anyone say a word. Not one word. She's nervous enough already. I'll hide the dress. Lucky I brought the turquoise one down to show you. I don't mind wearing it to avoid spoiling my sister's day. She'll only find out at the church and she'll be swept along with it all by then. Don't any of you spoil my big sister's big day.'

Chris Rowe

October 29

Playtime

The sun was low, red against a pale sky that was almost green in the half-light. As the temperature dropped, ice began to form in the puddles left by the previous night's storm. The country park closed at four o'clock and all the visitors had left more than an hour ago. The house was closed too, inhabited only by the cleaners and security guards, who kept it clean and safe until the morning. The family was wintering in the Caribbean, away from the cold and the public.

The playground, tucked away in a small corner, was cut off from the rest of the park by a thick tangle of rhododendrons. A stream wound its way in and out of the woods, swollen by the rain, its trilling and gurgling the only sounds in the still twilight until a car engine shattered the quiet. Its headlights raked over the wood and rope play apparatus, stark against the fading light. In the deepening twilight the swings with their old tyres and thick ropes tied to a rough wooden crossbeam with huge knots took on a more macabre appearance, like giant nooses depending from a gallows. One of the tyres still moved gently, as if a departing child couldn't resist one last shove.

The jungle gym, full of interesting shapes for children to climb over and under, loomed menacingly behind, a piece of perverse machinery used by aliens to manufacture hideous beings. Beneath it, in the bark that was alleged to cushion any fall, lay a small red ball, hardly visible now as the sky darkened to navy. The moon was early, a small slice hanging above Venus.

Two pale figures appeared by the slide. Gradually the shapes became children, a girl and a boy, insubstantial in the gloom. She wore an elaborate white dress with a full skirt, longer than was fashionable, and her fair hair hung down to her waist. He was dressed in a curiously formal suit and was as pale as the moon. All the colour had been drained out of the pair, who stood motionless, hand in hand, listening and waiting. The car disappeared into the distance and the children moved, as if suddenly freed. Their voices shrill in the quiet, they chased each other round the swings and the jungle gym, jumping and laughing in their excitement. They clambered in and out of the wooden shapes, up and down the slide, and then ran over to the swings. Instead of swinging, they wriggled through the tyres, treating them like an obstacle course, but they soon tired of that game.

The boy saw the ball and pointed at it. The girl came and stood by his side. He bent down to pick it up, but his hand did not connect. The ball lay where it had fallen. She, too, tried to pick it up, but again it stayed on the ground. A look passed between them and they ran away to the far end of the playground. There was no gate or fence barring their way, but they stopped still for a moment and then turned back. They raced around and around, laughing and shouting once more, until exhausted, they stopped by the oak tree where they had first appeared. Then she took his hand and slowly they faded into the night.

Fran Neatherway

October 30

Night Watching

The corridor was gloomy, long, and very narrow. The floor creaked underfoot, and the low ceiling was festooned with dust-filled webs. The only door was on the left at the far end, and the end wall hosted a small, dark, stained-glass window of purples, deep reds, and golden-syrup hues, that let in very little light; just a strange shifting indefinite pattern that fled across the carpet and flickered over one small patch of wall.

The door stood ajar, but only by a finger-width, and a faint green glow emanated. Isla pushed the door wider, took in the beautiful green décor, and the late afternoon sun pouring in through the tall french-windows. There was a balcony beyond the glass, and two pots of summer planting stood to either side on the stone floor.

"Ah! You're here." The voice made her jump and she turned to see a short, plump, bald man standing in the doorway, smiling.

"I'm Hermann," he said, shoving his hands nervously into his pockets. "I'm the Organizer for this weekend."

Isla moved her case off the chair and indicated he could sit. Instead he went to look out over the balcony rail.

"Last year was good fun. I made new friends," and he waved to someone she couldn't see.

Somewhere a gong sounded. Dinner. Hermann shot off without another word, and Isla carefully closed the french-windows and locked the room as she left. She realised she didn't know where to go next, and Hermann was already out of sight! The long creepy corridor seemed shorter this time, and on the staircase many people were chattering away, working their way down to the hall. Although she peered at all the faces, Isla recognised no-one. She didn't know whether to be relieved or disappointed.

The food was good, her fellow diners were friendly, and very soon they were all sharing experiences, advice, and laughing about their mistakes or how they'd been spooked.

"So there I was," said Gavin, "it was totally dark, but I knew there were others fairly close, I just couldn't see them any longer. I heard rustlings, and twigs snapping, but I kept telling myself that sounds always seem louder at night. I have to admit I was getting a bit jumpy. And then 'The Noise' started. I can't even describe it, it was so unreal. It went on and on, and now I really was scared. I was ready to run, but no longer had any idea which way! I couldn't even pinpoint that hellish sound. Then it stopped. But so had all the other sounds.

"It came again. Closer this time, and all around me! Suddenly a hand fell on my shoulder." Gavin paused for dramatic effect. "It was our Co-Ordinator. He said the watch was being called off. It had been a no-show at all points. I was gibbering by then, but managed to ask about that noise," another pause, "Turned out it was just nightjars!!"

Everyone was laughing when Hermann got to his feet and said to the room, "Get your coats, and whatever gear you've brought with you, and we'll go walkabout in the Old Hall, and Abbey ruins. No torches, people, it destroys your night vision. You've got fifteen minutes. Meet outside the front door."

The hum of excited voices tailed off into the distance as Isla ran up to her room, grabbed her coat, and ran back. Hermann was the only person standing at the door.

"Sorry you're way out down the long corridor, but we had to emergency house some poor camping families who'd lost their tents. As you were on your own, it seemed best to put you in the green bedroom."

"It's OK," Isla smiled. "It's beautiful. But such a long corridor for one room? Seems odd."

"There are rooms, but the doors are boarded over. The rooms aren't currently usable, the whole wing was in a terrible state, just that stained-glass window was in perfect condition. Very mysterious."

Behind them the others were excitedly gathering.

"Right," said Hermann "Detectors at the ready, and off to the ruins we go."

EE Blythe

October 31

Tricked A Treat

It's not quicker using the self-checkout tills, everyone knows that. I have reached that conclusion on countless supermarket ordeals. I even conducted a scientific test once; I split the shopping with my husband and instructed him to queue behind the longest line at the tills, whilst I headed for the self checkouts. He was relaxing in the cafe, sipping a cappuccino, by the time I stumbled along, exasperation etched indelibly across my entire face.

And when you are in a tearing hurry, the temptation to bypass the human option and whizz through via 'automation' is, bizarrely, even greater. It is not until you have heard "Approval needed" and "Unexpected item in bagging area, please remove this item" half a dozen times, that it dawns on you that you have made the mistake you vowed never to make again last time you were in a tearing hurry!

I found myself in this very situation on the last day of October. I was late leaving work, the traffic was horrendous, I had promised to take my son to his mate's house for a party and we were expecting friends round for drinks and nibbles - neither of which were much evident in our kitchen cupboards. I raced down the aisles, swerved round awkwardly parked trolleys, squeezed through knots of conversing pensioners, grabbing snacks, almost at random, from the shelves and headed for the checkouts. The queues, as I approached with my overloaded, overweight basket, seemed longer and slower than ever, so I charged towards a vacant self-checkout terminal, skidding to a halt just in front of an elderly gentleman wielding two bottles of red wine. With what I hoped was an apologetic and explanatory glance in his direction, I slammed my basket down and started to scan.

"Welcome to Self-checkout, please press Start." My first three items were hastily returned to the basket, I did as I was instructed and started - again. "Please scan your first item." Yes, ok, that much is obvious!

At the first bottle of wine: "Approval needed." When I eventually caught the eye of the young assistant, he ambled, casually, over and waved his magic card in front of the screen. And yes, I had another bottle of wine which surfaced three items later!

After a smooth flow of half a dozen or so more items, I was again stalled. "Unexpected item..." I looked aghast at the chaotic heap of crisps, dips and wine bottles strewn across the bagging area. What was the last thing I scanned? A bunch of grapes, right, did that scan? Yes, but that was not the previous item, the last item was a pack of mini-pork pies. I picked it up, and put it down again. "Unexpected item...." I picked it up and put it down again - firmly. "Unexpected item..." I picked it up and placed it - firmly and deliberately - on the surface of the bagging area. "Unexpected item..." I picked up other items and hurled them forcefully on the surface of the bagging area. "Unexpected item..."

I turned to catch the eye of the young assistant, hoping my pleading glance would bring him over with his magic card at more than a casual amble. He ambled, casually, over and, before I could explain the cause of my panic, waved his magic card in front of the screen.

After a smooth period of scanning which lasted all of 30 seconds - "Unexpected item..." and the whole palaver of trying to identify the unexpected item was repeated, but with an increased measure of panic and desperation. I must now have been creating quite a scene, as several customers paused from their trouble-free scanning and cast me suspicious sideways glances. The young assistant ambled purposefully over - of his own accord - and enquired if I needed assistance. I started to blurt out a confused explanation. He just scratched his head and waved his magic card in front of the screen. I had only one more item, it was a bottle of wine!

I paid - how can the machine remain so calm and polite? Yes, all right, I know - it's a machine. I crammed my shopping into three carrier bags and turned my back on the terminal as it calmly and politely thanked me for using... As I rushed for the exit I noticed an elderly gentleman standing nonchalantly by the local adverts board. He held a bag which seemed to contain just two bottles of wine. As I hurried by, I noticed his rather striking waistcoat, a deep, midnight blue, emblazoned with yellow moon and star motifs. With his free hand he was tucking away what seemed to be a short stick or rod into the inside pocket of his velvet jacket. I'm sure he winked as I passed; a brief, very wry smile passed across his face, vanished almost as soon as it appeared. As I ventured out into a cold, blustery rain squall, I looked back over my shoulder, but the elderly gentleman had completely disappeared.

Steve Redshaw

November

November 1

Scary Movies

Diane and David were getting quite adventurous. Things had been a little slow lately, so David had decided to spice up their Friday nights with a series of horror films.

They had never dabbled before; there was something slightly unsettling about spookiness, and something rather stomach-churning about gore. They preferred a good Jane Austen adaptation, a bit of Judi Dench or - at a push - Hugh Grant.

David did the research and came up with some goodies on Netflix. It was Stephen King's disturbing scare-fest with a sinister clown living in the sewers. That should put us on edge, he thought, and he followed it up with Insidious, a traditional haunted house movie with all the usual horror film trappings - a calm start, a family in a new house, strange things start happening, a medium arrives, things get worse and a final confrontation with the evil thingy.

At one point, Diane had to hide behind her sewing and David pretended to be engrossed in the television listings rather than give full attention to the spine-chilling scene evolving in front of their eyes. But the change in mood had the desired effect when bedtime came. Having double-checked the locks before retiring, David got a win-bonus beneath the sheets when Diane needed some reassurance after the lights went out.

So far, so good. But just after two, David woke with a start. Laughter? No, surely. Even his nocturnal neighbours would be asleep by now. Footsteps? Like a child running about? Their daughter Phoebe had long left home, her bedroom now turned into a hobby room, mini-gym and shelf storage for David's collection of vintage car badges.

David rose to investigate. It had been a long time since he'd given up his ventriloquist act. Mr Chuckles was in retirement, safely locked away in his wooden box on the top shelf. Or was he? As he opened the door of the spare room, a head slowly turned towards him and a pair of eyes looked in his direction. Mr Chuckles wanted to play.

John Howes

November 2

The Small Square Space

The wall opened up, slowly, revealing a dimly lit space behind. He looked back over his shoulder. There was no-one there. No-one to stop him, no-one to see, no-one to follow him. He paused one more second before stepping through the gap. He expected the doorway to close as silently as it had opened, but it didn't.

He was now standing in a small squarish shape, completely empty, with no visible lighting, and nowhere to sit. Without turning round he stepped back through the opening. He'd seen enough *Dr Who* and horror films to know that moving further into the room could well close the doorway, and there'd be no way to open it from the inside.

He kept walking backwards until the wall closed up again. Silently. Seamlessly. Intrigued, he moved forwards again, but this time nothing happened. Close inspection of the wall showed no indication that there had ever been a doorway. He swallowed hard. What was happening here? He stood transfixed.

"You in here, Larry?" Stephanie's voice jolted him back to reality, and as she rounded the corner, she asked if he'd found anything interesting. With a last look at the unblemished wall, he shook his head, and held out his arms to encompass the empty area.

"No, this is no use for filming" she said, and was gone again. Relieved, he followed her. He knew that if she'd triggered the strange door, she would have rushed straight in. Stephanie was like that. And he knew, with certainty, that she would have been trapped in the little square room, that he now thought of as The Oubliette.

What he didn't know was that the small square space had not been empty.

EE Blythe

November 3

Bonfire Night

When did you become so small? It seems like only yesterday I was perched on your shoulders, taller than the trees, screaming in both fear and delight and here we are today. I'm helping you brush your teeth, moving you across the bed, calling for the nurses to help. How did this happen?

Time it seems has slipped by and left behind a shadow of who you were.

One minute we were scrumping for apples across the road at Mrs Brown's. I had never seen her but heard that if she caught you stealing, she would cast a spell that would turn you into a tree and be fixed forever in her orchard, unable to bear even fruit.

'Rubbish,' you said. 'Listen, this is how we do it. We go around the back. I lift you over and you run amongst the trees, filling the bag. Then, quickly, you come back to the wall, toss the bag to me, reach up and I will pull you back over the wall.' Seemed like a good plan and it worked. Despite my pounding heart and my momentary shock at the size of her orchard.

+   +

And my heart pounds heavily now as my sister asks me to pull your arms up, raising you on the bed. No nurses in sight and you are all slumped. Your wrists are thin and tired. I can feel the bones in your back. Where is the flesh? How did this happen?

You only came to one Parent Teachers Association meeting. My chest could have burst with pride when you walked into the class wearing your RAF uniform. My, how gorgeous you looked. So tall and strong. Miss Ruddiger was quite flustered by your presence.

'The trouble with your daughter,' she started, 'is that she is more interested in boys than studies...'

I remember how you looked at me. Sheer horror and shame. Was

Miss Ruddiger fair? Maybe I did lead the boys to torment her. She was so dull, dull, dull. We would convince her to enter the walk-in cupboard to get some much-needed article to enable us to complete our work. We were always running out of paper and pens at these opportune moments. I would get Jamie T to place the *Chambers Dictionary* on top of the wedged door and we would wait for her to push it open and, kapow, land on her head. Somehow that seemed funny aged seven. I found out much later she died aged 40 of breast cancer. I wonder if all those dictionaries falling on her head had anything to do with her getting cancer so young? She had spent all of her life living with her mother who then outlived her. She really must have hated us. Still, I never forgave her for saying that to you...

Saturday nights – football signature tune plays as we serve up salad sandwiches with Marks and Spencer peanuts. They used to be so big. Large, salty and only consumed as football played. We bought you some recently and you were disappointed.

'When did these become so small?' you say, holding one up in disgust. 'And look, they're not even American anymore, they're Chinese.'

The dialysis machine whirrs around you. Every now and again the green light on top of the machine goes amber, sometimes red. Nurses approach – not rushed or panicked, like the feeling in my chest. I'm not medical but is blood pressure of forty over eighty even possible? They don't seem phased. I try to stay calm and notice I am talking too much again.

Forty over eighty for some reason makes me think of aliens... Would a world with Zombies be possible? We are sitting side by side, watching *The Walking Dead*. I think it became boring by season six. You look at me and say, no, it's just getting interesting. It's at the point where they can trust no-one. Human nature is playing out.

+   +

Can I trust these nurses? These consultants. 'We will be with you all the way'. All the way where?

+   +

I want to tell you about that bonfire night... but you are sleeping. Do you remember it? We couldn't afford to buy the tickets. We didn't have a garden, so I had gone round the back to my posh neighbour's holiday house and I was perched on their garden wall, looking at the silhouette of the fire.

You came outside and said, 'Do you want to go?'

'Yes,' I said.

'We can go like commandos, in camouflage, across the golf course. We'll have to make sure we're not spotted. We can use the bunkers as shelters... are you up for it?'

'Yes I am,' I said. My apple scrumping training had prepared me for this mission.

+   +

We set off. It is pitch black. You have a torch but use it sparingly in case the enemy picks up its glow. We have to get from the first tee to the eighth, unnoticed. You know the course inside out. I don't and it's so deadly dark. I trust you as we set off into the night, throwing ourselves into the bunkers and around the gorse. Every time I gasp or giggle you tell me to be quiet in case our mission is scuppered. Finally, we lie, backs in the sand of the bunker, looking up at the sky and watch the firework display. It is magnificent. The noise and the colours. And we are invincible. Do you remember, Dad? Do you remember?

You're asleep now. I kiss you and tell you I love you. Leaving the hospital I can hear a Catherine wheel somewhere in the sky. It's the Queen's 90th birthday.

I stop and look up. I can see it in the distance. In this moment it fills the sky with colour. It's magnificent. Strong, soaring, invincible. Swirling bright and furious for a few more seconds before it starts to fade, quietly, getting smaller and smaller before disappearing into the darkness forever.

Fiona White

November 4

The Last Bonfire

The bonfire on the rough ground was getting taller, day by day, and the local children were proud of their efforts and looking forward to bonfire night. The heart of the growing woodpile was an old bedside cabinet, stuffed full with broken-up branches that had been brought down in the huge storm before HallowE'en, and the gaps filled with old jumpers that they'd scrounged at the Scouts' jumble sale. For weeks running up to bonfire night the children had been out scavenging what they could, knocking on doors and asking for anything to burn, and collecting as much combustible material as they could carry away from the riverside.

Then disaster struck. A rival gang of bonfire builders raided their stack, and apart from the cabinet, anything that would burn for a reasonable length of time had been purloined. This called for extreme measures.

The boys had a plan, but as the girls pointed out, it was illegal. Raiding a nearby building site was too risky, but, they told the scowling lads, 'There's nothing to stop us asking for anything they don't want', which is what they did !

The man sawing planks in front of the new block of flats was dressed in dusty blue from head to foot. Dungarees, shirt, jacket and hat had once been a deep blue, but now, after years of use and washing, they were no longer vivid, and they were all, even the hat, liberally coated in cement dust and concrete. He looked up as the gaggle of youngsters arrived, and peered at them through pale eyes as dusty blue as his clothes. He stepped right in front of them, stopping them dead in their track. One of the girls was pushed forward: 'Go on, it was your idea'. She took a deep breath and asked if there were any unwanted bits of wood they could have for their bonfire, as someone had stolen most of theirs in the night.

The man thought for a bit, weighing them up, then pointed with his saw at a large heap of mixed items towards the back of the building site.

'Help yourself from that pile, but only that pile. And don't go telling everyone, I've got work to get on with. Can't keep stopping for kids' bonfires,' and he grinned.

Straight away the children could see broken scaffolding planks in the pile, so pulled those out first to carry them back. While lugging the thick, heavy planking back home they were spotted by another group gathering tinder, who asked them where they'd got the wood from. Hurrying on, they said nothing. Worried that these prize finds would be spirited away again, they decided to stash them in Anthony's garden shed and just bring them out on the afternoon of the fire. The rest they put onto the heap.

On the morning of the bonfire, the boys went back to the building site for one last haul, but no-one was there. The compound, however, was not locked up, and there were more scaffolding planks, full-size scaffolding planks, on one edge of the heap. So they helped themselves to this bounty.

The bonfire was magnificent; tall and wide and solid, and it burned for hours. There were baked potatoes and fat pork sausages, brought out by the mothers, while the men took charge of feeding the bonfire and lighting a few fireworks. As per tradition, the Catherine Wheel flew off its nail, hurriedly shifting part of the crowd in alarm, Jumping-Jacks chased screaming children, and the small-fry nearly set fire to their mittens while waving sparklers. The young adults stayed by the fire, long into the night, and the embers were still warm in the frosty morning.

It was the last bonfire the neighbourhood would have on that patch of rough ground. A Methodist church was going to be built there the following year. End of an era, some said.

During the next week, the "bush telegraph" delivered the news that expensive scaffolding planks had mysteriously gone from the site for the new building.						**EE Blythe**

I'm not saying that this story is all true, but then, I'm not saying it's all fantasy!

November 5

Don't Forget The Skylarks

November 5th 2005

It was a cold and windy evening. Judy was standing with her eyes closed and her hands stuffed deep into her coat pockets; she was wearing a hat pulled down over her forehead, a scarf and gloves, her feet were cold and she couldn't stop shivering. The explosions made her jump and the smoke from the fire was burning her eyes, which was fine because she was crying. She hadn't wanted to come to the party, she had never liked fireworks, they frightened her. She had been hit by one as a child and her coat had caught fire; only her fast thinking father had saved her from serious burns.

Felicity, her eldest and very bossy daughter, had insisted that she come out. "You can't sit indoors all day waiting for news, Mum," she had said. "Come out, even if it's only for an hour, it will do you good."

Judy felt that nothing would do her good at the moment. She was holding tightly to her mobile phone, which was inside her glove so that she would feel it vibrate. It had vibrated once already that day, around two o'clock, when the message had read; Don't Forget The Skylarks.

At first she had been confused. "What the...?" she had thought, then she had remembered and the crying had started. She knew that the next vibration would change her life for ever.

Linda Slate

November 6

Bonfire

"Rain, rain, go away, come again another day."

We'd been chanting the rhyme all week, but with no luck. It was still raining. Sheets of rain had teemed down for eight days, soaking everything. The brook had overflowed, drowning the corn fields, and the village green was a quagmire. The small stream running down the middle of our road was growing bigger every day. We wore wellies whenever we went out and ran to school jumping in the puddles and splashing each other. Our mums complained bitterly about our wet, muddy clothing and despaired of ever having dry washing again.

We'd been collecting wood and old rubbish since the end of September. It was going to be the biggest and best bonfire ever, if the rain stopped for long enough for it to burn. Luckily we had been covering the growing heap with an old tarpaulin every night and everybody had their fingers crossed that it'd be dry enough come Saturday. We regarded Mr. Watkins with awe after he'd given us the tarpaulin and suggested that we use it to keep the bonfire dry. None of us could remember such a wet November, but then none of us could remember further back than seven years ago, apart from Kevin Phelps who swore blind he could remember the coronation party, even though he was only nine months old at the time.

We all had our fireworks ready, in old biscuit tins for safety, but we weren't allowed to set them off. That privilege was reserved for our dads, who also decided precisely when the bonfire would be lit. We could only have sparklers. The older boys always managed to get hold of bangers and jumping jacks, which they threw at the girls, who screamed and giggled and tossed their hair and pretended to be above such childish games. We'd look longingly at the bangers and every year beg our mums to buy us some, but they always refused. We couldn't wait to be thirteen so we could buy our own.

Bonfire Night fell on the Saturday that year, which meant we could all stay up late. The previous week had been half term and we had driven our mums mad with whining about the weather and demanding things to do. We couldn't go and collect more wood because it was too wet and wouldn't burn.

The older girls were making the guy, same as always, and there was much giggling and secrecy about it. No-one ever saw it until the last moment when it suddenly materialised on top of the bonfire just before it was set alight. It was the tradition in our village for the guy to resemble one of the local notables. Last year it had been the schoolmaster's turn. Fortunately for all concerned, he did not live in the village and therefore never saw the glee that greeted his fiery death.

A week is a long time for a ten year old, especially when there is something exciting to look forward to. Bonfire Night was one of the highlights of our year, along with Christmas, Easter and birthdays. The fireworks lit up the sky and dazzled us with their beauty. Rockets soared into the night, almost touching the stars, and exploded into showers of golden rain. Roman candles produced streams of liquid light and volcanoes sprayed red fires. Catherine Wheels spun and whirled, scattering gold and silver sparks. Traffic lights changed from red to amber to green, amazing us with their cleverness. We waved our sparklers enthusiastically as we wrote our names in the air. It was always over far too soon, but then we could watch the bonfire burn until bedtime. We could hardly wait.

At last Saturday arrived and we grew more and more excited. The rain had suddenly stopped on Friday afternoon and an east wind had sprung up. Our mums said it was good drying weather and promptly hung the washing out. We just hoped it would be good burning weather and kept going to check on the bonfire. Eventually our dads forbade any of us to go near it, as we kept prodding and poking at it. They were afraid one of us would bring the whole thing down. We spent the afternoon hanging around, getting underfoot and in the way. The village green was pretty squelchy, but the brook was subsiding and the stream no longer ran down the middle of the road. We still needed our wellies, though. The younger children were sent to bed for a couple of hours in the afternoon and the older ones helped with making soup and scrubbing potatoes for baking in the ashes of the fire.

At about half past six everyone started putting on their coats and wellies and drifting back outside. Although there was never a fixed time for lighting the bonfire, we all knew somehow when the time had come. It was a cold clear night, dry with a bit of a breeze. The girls were just bringing the guy out for his sacrifice. As soon as we saw it, we all knew who it was supposed to be. It had red hair and a beard and was dressed in black with a white collar round its neck. There were a few shocked gasps and surprised giggles as traditionally the vicar was never used for the guy, Bonfire Night still being a bit of a pagan festival. The vicar was new that year and had put quite a few backs up as he proceeded to change everything he could get his hands on, from the flower rota to Matins. Ours was not a village that liked change.

The girls handed the guy to our dads who removed the tarpaulin and placed it on top of the bonfire. The vicar himself looked unamused, but the old vicar had never attended the bonfire and didn't interfere with our traditions. Our dads got out the matches and firelighters and attempted to light the fire, but it refused to catch. One of them shouted that it was still too damp and someone else hurried off to get some paraffin, which was then poured over the bonfire. It still wouldn't light. People started to get restless and we could hear the vicar laughing with his wife.

'That'll teach them to try and burn a man of the cloth,' he chortled.

Then, as we were all wondering whether to light our fireworks, the wind died down and the air became still and heavy. There was a loud crash of thunder and the sky was split by a huge bolt of lightning, striking the ground in the next field. Another flash lit up the whole sky, and, as the thunder rolled, the bonfire blazed up. The girls' screams were followed by silence as we took in what had happened. Then the rain began, soaking us in seconds as we all ran for cover. The bonfire continued to burn, in spite of the heavy downpour, until all that was left was a large charred circle. Our dads covered it with earth, saying they had to make sure the fire was really out.

In church the next morning the vicar didn't mention the bonfire or the storm, and neither did anyone else. We set our fireworks off that evening, but our hearts weren't in it. The big boys didn't even bother to throw their bangers. The following year by an unspoken communal decision, there was no guy on the bonfire and there never has been since.

Fran Neatherway

November 7

Guy Fawkes' Night

'Hi, Karen, I'll be there in...' She shifted the phone momentarily from ear to eye-view. 'Oh fifteen minutes. Yea, s'me here, Cathy. Only I'll be five minutes late, had to get the cat all safely gathered in. Then had to go back to check I'd locked the cat-flap. You know what it's like on Bonfire Night. Little Ghengie wouldn't get over it if she escaped. He loves Venom. Yeh, I know – but he insisted – Ghengie absolutely and utterly refused to call it anything else. Bit embarrassing at the vet's but then I pay enough. Anyway, what's in a name, eh? as the Bard said.'

Carefully placing her door key in her inside pocket, she set off with little Ghengie trotting, as he usually did, obediently alongside as his mother's cloud of words floated away over his head and out of his hearing, punctuated this time by occasional premature bangs and fizzings set off by impatient celebrants.

'So, you did say, didn't you, there'd be food – sausages and buns? What! Gluten free veggie-burgers, as well. Organic! Wow! This is a real trendy area I'm in!

'So, Ghengie's wearing a white hat. Like me, so I can spot him just in case in the dark. Must be a careful parent.' She giggled. 'But no, I hope I do take my responsibility as his parent seriously. So look out for us, two white tops, so - ooh I can see you now, Karen. Far off, over by the gate, bright yellow scarf high up and two, also yellow, scarves, lower down, either side – Tarquin and Bouddica. Lucky the three of them get on so well together. I think they looked after Gheng when he started school. No one's ever tried to bully him. Even though he's so quiet. Not outgoing like your two. They live up to their names, but Ghenghis was so wrong for him. That phase we all had for tough names meaning tough kids. Thank goodness Nigel and I split before a second came along. His mother had started dropping hints about Heathcliff if a boy. I ask you! Imagine me at my door yelling "Heathcliff!" down the street.

Specially with my name. It was to be Attila if a girl. Yea, she got that wrong, ignorant b. Anyway I knocked that idea on the head. Got a budgie, a hen, and called that Attila. Yea?'

Ghengie's head shot up at the mention of the budgie, a well-loved pet, whom he was careful to keep out of the clutches of his beloved Venom. Ghenghis enforced harmony.

His mother switched her phone off as Karen came alongside. They stood near the unanimated bonfire, waiting.

In truth her friend's children found Ghengie an easy-going companion. Ghenghis was a watching child, self-contained, with little to say for himself, but he noticed things that they never did and directed their attention to things they would otherwise have missed. It was just one step away from telling them what to see and what to think. Within two weeks they had become his protectors: within two months they were his loyal henchmen.

Ghenghie's ears were used to inattention but his eyes soon became fire-focused. Near him a piece of blackened wood like dark, touch-tempting velvet had curved and split into lumps with regular fissures. One end had the outline of an orange glow. A log beside it spurted sudden jets of white flares, with roaring, poofing sounds. He tried to time its next outburst. Behind it, ever-changing orange sheets of flame flapped into curves both sinuous and jagged. He tried to guess where the next flame would appear and how high it would dance. He smelt the potent mixture of wood burning (no plastic consumed in this fire) and the enticing aroma of roasting, organic of course, pork. Time passed unnoticed until he became aware of his mother's voice and the phone she was flourishing aloft.

'Fireworks look. I'll try and see'f I c'n photo them on the phone. Gheng an I c'n look at 'em later. I'll have to put it on the laptop first for him. He won't look at anything on my phone.' Years later Boudicca would teasingly call him phone phobic.

The fireworks came to a glorious, dazzling final flourish with reverberating booms and staccato crackling. The vegan sausages and olive-oil fried organic onions were all consumed. People dispersed.

Torches on phones lit the way around the tussocky field. The friends, still hungry, decided to walk to the nearest fish and chip shop.

'They serve them in newspaper, not real papers, of course, not hygienic but so nostalgic.' After buying, the friends parted.

Not long after: 'Hi, Cathy here. No, we're not eating on the way back. Gheng likes to enjoy the smell as long as possible. We'll have them at home on the table.'

They did and were soon looking at a pile of the remnants of their repast.

'Whew I'm bushed,' said Cathy, for the first time to herself and not the phone. She lit up for a rare, relaxing cigarette, but decided a bathroom visit was necessary first. Ghenghis the Watcher was still feasting his imagination remembering the flames – the soft whooshes, sparks cracking and spitting, that alluring dancing fluidity of the flames.

After a meal you put things in the sink, so he did: the so-called newspaper (fake news indeed) and the greaseproof paper. But you couldn't wash these so he took his mother's lighter and flicked it at the edge of a wrapper, watching it turn blue. Would it take? Would it? He saw a corner bloom yellow. He added the polystyrene trays and watched them begin to writhe and shrivel into a nasty-smelling slime. Then like some sacrificing pagan priest, from table to sink he solemnly bore the phone to lower it onto its pyre.

Chris Rowe

November 8

Why I Love Newspapers

Much of my working life was spent as a journalist producing local newspapers and you might think that, by now, I would be fed up with them - but I never am.

I am still excited to pick up an unread newspaper: its neatness, its satisfyingly rectangular shape, the thickness of the different sections. All those pages promise interest, challenging opinions and new ideas, new ways of seeing the world and a window into other people's lives.

At the moment, I have *The Sunday Times* delivered and love to spread its reading throughout the week. Starting with either the sport or news section, I gradually work through my favourite parts and favourite columnists... Rod Liddell, Camilla Long and even Jeremy Clarkson. After the news section, I move to the culture supplement and read reviews of television, film, radio and books. The television listings are then handy for the week ahead.

Next, I go to the glossy magazine, often the least satisfying part of the paper and then, if I have time, the business, money and travel sections. Sometimes these are left in my newspaper basket and find themselves recycled without having their pages turned.

On holiday, my treat is to get a newspaper every day. I usually vary between *The Times* and *The Guardian*. If I'm getting behind in my reading, I will sometimes go for *The i*, a handy digest without making too many demands on one's time. By the end of the holiday week, the floor of our cottage or apartment is covered with discarded sections, inserts, magazines and supplements. That suggests it has been a pretty good week.

But on a recent holiday in Derbyshire, we stayed in such a remote location that a newspaper was very hard to come by. We tried the nearest village but they said we would have to order one in advance. When we visited a town nearby, it turned out there wasn't even a newsagent and someone in the post office suggested we try another town several miles away. When I eventually got my hands on *The Times*, it felt like uncovering a golden nugget. I clung on for dear life and ended up reading nearly every word.

It may be simpler and quicker to click on a link and read a news story online, and I often do this, especially when something big is breaking and I am keen for a quick update. However, can anything replace the satisfaction of a freshly-printed unread newspaper, the work of dozens, maybe hundreds of journalists who have laboured over every word, discussed every punctuation mark and considered carefully which photographs to choose and how to present them? Value your local and national newspapers while you can. You will miss them if they disappear.

John Howes

November 9

You Had To Be There

'And everyone fell about laughing,' Paul said, in a fit of giggles himself. His friends Ben and Luke just looked at each other.

It was well into the evening do of their mate's wedding, and the three of them were having a good catch up over a pint.

'I don't get what's so funny,' Ben said.

'Where did the cow come into it?' Luke asked.

'Cow?' Paul queried, his laughter ceasing at this weird question.

'Yes. You said there was a dog and a cow.'

'No, I said the dog was called Cal. C A L.'

'Oh. What a stupid name for a dog.'

'It was short for something. I can't remember now. As I said, it wasn't my dog.'

'What wasn't your dog?' Keith said, sitting down at the table with a fresh drink in his hand.

'I'm telling them how I met my wife,' Paul explained.

'What's that got to do with a dog?' Keith asked.

'I met my wife with a dog.'

'You can't say that!' Marie said, appearing behind Paul.

'Can't say what?'

'You can't call your wife a dog.'

'No, I said I met her with a dog. I used to borrow my mate's dog. He was this cute little thing. Women loved it.'

'Like some tiny, furry wingman,' Keith said with a grin.

'Yeah,' Paul replied, glad that someone was seeing the funny side.

'Why was this bloke Benny drawing it, though?' Luke asked.

'What?' Paul said, completely taken aback by the question.

'You said there was some bloke called Benny Hill who was drawing you all running.'

'No, I said us running down the street was like a Benny Hill sketch,'

Paul said, wanting to bang his head on the table.

'Oh. Who's Benny Hill?'

'You know. He did those comedy sketches back in the seventies or something.'

All of Paul's friends had blank expressions.

'Why were you running?' Marie asked.

Paul took a breath. He wished he'd never started.

'I used to take my mate's dog for a walk to chat up women. That was how I met my Jane. She loved the dog. She seemed to like me. Then I accidentally dropped the lead and the dog raced off -'

'Cow the dog,' Luke said with a knowing smile.

'Cal the dog!' Paul corrected, shaking his head. 'Cal! The dog ran off, I ran after him, Jane ran after me, then her mates started running after her -'

'Was he from the paper or something?' Ben asked.

'Who?'

'This Benny man who was drawing you.'

'No, he wasn't... Us running was like a Benny Hill sketch. You know, with the music.'

'Like a cartoonist?'

Paul exhaled sharply. 'No. Look. It was really funny. Clearly you had to be there. I caught up with the dog, Jane caught up with me, and...'

Paul looked at the bewildered faces of his friends. Why did they not understand? It had been one of the funniest things ever to happen to him.

'And...'

They waited for him to finish, as if there was a punchline coming that might explain why the story needed telling. Paul would never be telling it again.

'And...'

He needed this conversation to end.

'And everyone fell about laughing. Another drink?'

Lindsay Woodward

November 10

No Room With A View

Sri Lanka was the destination for our Leopard Research Project in November 2003. We were totally isolated 29 kilometres from India in the middle of the Indian Ocean with no escape. Brenda, an ex-navy wife friend, and I felt abandoned on the exotic island with the airport closed and a coup declared, 5,445 miles from home.

There had been a sudden overthrow of the government when the Sri Lankan President had sacked several ministers, including her prime minister, while he was visiting George W. Bush in Washington.

We travelled in our minibus to the Yala Safari Park, on the south easterly corner of the tear-drop shaped island of Serendipity. We saw protesters speeding the other way towards the airport in Colombo. They were hanging out of jeeps and cars making a terrific din, peeping horns, shouting, and shaking their tightly clenched fists threateningly at us.

Eventually we arrived at our hot, tropical holiday destination and decided to take a leisurely swim in the large, outdoor pool. Life carried on. Floating on my back, in a world of my own, I attempted to dismiss worrying thoughts of any troubles in the north.

Would they send in RAF planes? I doubted it.

We returned to our accommodation. Our room was dark, cool and basic with a fan whizzing around high in the ceiling, closed shutters keeping out the scorching sun, dark wooden floors, light brown counterpanes patterned with large brown leaves. Simple, colourless décor.

I pulled back the shutters to reveal our view. Two dogs were leisurely strolling across a line of rocks in the middle of a still, tree-reflected water. All was calm, as our fears and worries momentarily disappeared. Fortunately, the 22 month cease-fire was respected.

The following year, Boxing Day, 2004 at 8 am when visiting my elder sister in Johannesburg, she greeted us with the devastating news of a

Sri Lankan Tsunami. Disaster… sixty visitors and only two water buffaloes were killed. Sadly, our low-rise hotel accommodation flattened.

Our Room with a View had been completely washed away.

No Room with a View.

Kate A Harris

November 11

A Moving Romance

She stared out of the window. Term had been a slog. She yearned for a glimpse of the red Midland clay – and there it was – soon be home now.

A presentable young man got on and sat opposite her. She was attractive and he'd soon started chatting. He was setting out his stall well, impressing her, he could see, as he told her all about his job. Luckily he remembered he should ask her about herself – it always went down well. Get on the train; get on with her, aha. Get off with her? Hm. He asked where she was going.

'Home. I'm a student.' When she said she was reading English, he began to talk about books, telling her his favourites. She responded and revealed she came from Nuneaton - like George Eliot.

'Yeah? Great writer. I like him,' he said, blowing his chances.

Her eyes went down to *Jane Eyre*, which she'd been reading when he'd got on. She muttered uh-uh to any further comments, bending her head well down. Brilliant read. Only hope that show-off creep opposite lets me get on with it. Great, he's getting off at Rugby.

The book soon had her engrossed: written romance was proving better than tricky reality. It made the time whizz until she became aware of the train's slowing into the station and looking up, saw the sign for Crewe.

Chris Rowe

November 12

My First Day At School

I have heard it said that they are the best years of our lives. But who says this? I do not know. For me, they were stressful and miserable.

I was born in Sutton Coldfield and my first five years were spent in a tied cottage on a farm. My mother took me to school on the cross bar of her bike with my little brother on the seat at the back. The first day we went in through a gate in the iron railings. There were two playgrounds, one for the younger children and the other for the older children. In my class, we had both four and five-year-olds. We had a reading book about a horse called Lob. I learned it off by heart but I never learned to read it

By lunchtime on the first day, I'd had enough so I tried to go home but I found the gate locked. I cried. I hadn't realised I didn't have a choice and I had to stay now every day! I didn't learn anything in this school.

Later we moved to a council house in Bannersgate with a new school just down the road. We had a proper bathroom! No more tin baths in front of the fire, no more out the back to the loo. It was a lovely new primary school. I soon caught up with reading and my brother was at the same school. We lived by Sutton Park and mother and father took us in there each weekend and my mother taught me all my birds, flowers and trees.

At 13, I went to Boldmere High School for girls. I was bullied until I learned to amuse the other girls. I must have had some good teachers but I remember sarcasm and criticism more. Life for me started when I left formal education.

Ruth Hughes

November 13

The Last Resort

Review of the Avernus Hotel.

Journey: *****
Very smooth, very efficient, very fast. Took the M25 to Heathrow and before I knew it, I was here. No hassles with traffic or parking or customs. Definitely 5 stars.

Accommodation: * Primitive.
Room seems to have been hacked out of rock. Thick wooden door with bars but good locks! No bedding or towels. No indoor plumbing. Haven't taken a shower since arrival. Tried complaining, but staff just sneered. Room service non-existent. No mobile phone signal, no Wi-Fi. And no mini-bar. Honestly, this is worse than that camping holiday when I was a kid. Rained all week. I'd never been so cold – not a problem here. It's very hot, much hotter than it's supposed to be, according to the brochure.

Shan't be staying here again.

Activities: * None so far.
Still waiting. Paid for boat trip, jet ski and winery visit. Not happened. No pool, just a horrible, murky lake. The water's red! Won't be swimming in there. The shore on the other side fire! No warning about wild fires in the brochure. Haven't seen daylight since I got here – the sky is covered by black billowing clouds of smoke.

And where are the lads? I said we should've gone to Prague or Amsterdam for Craig's stag weekend, but no, they all wanted to go to Italy. Didn't want to come. Don't want to go to his stupid wedding either.

Hen weekend went to a spa. I know they'll all get drunk and talk too much. If Stephanie finds out I shagged the bride and both bridesmaids, there'll be hell to pay. If Craig finds out, I'll be dead.

Don't want to accidentally post this last bit when I finally get a signal. Deleting it.

(Last two paragraphs deleted)

Staff: Null points!
Can't find the bar. Asked for a drink – staff ignore me. None of them seem to be working. And the uniforms – red bodysuits and weird masks. It's not Hallowe'en – that was two weeks ago! What's up with that? I've asked to speak to the manager, but they laughed at me. I've seen him walking about – tall, dark and handsome, if you like that sort of thing. Very expensive suit. He's coming this way. I'll be giving him a piece of my mind.

Oh.

Final Review:
Don't come here. You really don't want to be here. No-one wants to be here – not them, not him, and not me. Aaaaargh!

Avernus is the ancient name of a volcanic crater near Naples. According to Virgil's *Aeneid*, the ancient Romans believed it was the entrance to the Underworld.

Fran Neatherway

November 14

Box Brownie

Here we are, ankle deep in the sea, my Mum, my sister and me, with my dress tucked in my knickers.

My Mum is holding up the hem of her frock, her best one that comes out of the wardrobe, smelling of mothballs, on two occasions each year. The other is Christmas Day, when, at teatime, she envelops her frock in a wrap-around pinafore while she spreads the bread, slices tomatoes and cucumber, shares out the ham, the tinned peaches and Carnation milk, pours the tea and adds a few drops from a miniature bottle of whisky.

In a few seconds a wave will hit the back of her knees. She will lose her balance, let go of her skirt and reach out to my sister.

My sister's newly-permed hair is trying to escape an army of hairpins. She is struggling to hold it down, while her other hand is holding mine. She is missing her boyfriend. She doesn't say, but I have seen her kissing his photograph when she thought no-one was watching.

We are on the beach in Rhyl, where we go on the train every year for Dad's one week annual holiday. In June he takes pen and lined paper, and writes in his beautiful Copperplate handwriting, the nouns all capitalised, every letter perfectly aligned, as was drilled into him with a ruler on his knuckles. Every year the letter is the same: Full Board and One Room with a Double and a Single Bed, please. I am squeezed in with my sister. We always stay at the same boarding house, dine at the same table, eating our meal quietly at five o'clock sharp with other families, voices hushed over the plates. Mum has to take her ration book so that the landlady can use that week's coupons.

Dad wakes early and shakes the sand out of his turn-ups from yesterday's ritual burial. I get dressed quickly, and we set off along the breezy promenade, where the cast-iron shelters are already filling with old men. Dad buys his Daily Herald from the kiosk and a paper cone of cockles or shrimps from the fish stall. We walk back, dipping in fingers, licking off the vinegar and the taste of the sea.

After breakfast, Mum collects a packet of sandwiches from the landlady and stuffs our bathing costumes into her bag. Mine is knitted from odd balls of wool, in stripes of yellow and brown. We call it The Wasp. It first belonged to my sister, and I am yet to discover that it stretches down to my knees when heavy with water. Mum opens the front door to knock the sand out of our shoes into a flower pot in the tiny strip of garden, and off we go for another day on the beach, bucket and spade jangling.

So, here we are, doing what we came for, paddling in the shallows, all holding hands together to save each other from the waves. Out of sight, facing us, is Dad, trousers rolled up to his knees, knotted hanky on his head, false teeth slipping as he smiles. He clicks the shutter, immortalises us for future generations. He is happy, proud that we are enjoying the fun of the week's holiday for which he has saved all year.

And here comes the wave that makes us all cling together. We scream and laugh until we cry.

Wendy Goulstone

November 15

Grandpa's G&T

It's that time of the afternoon again. I do look forward to my G&T. Or should we call it the evening. This time of year the nights are drawing in with a vengeance. Do you know the temperature difference between today and yesterday? 15 degrees Centigrade! I was working on the allotment in my t-shirt yesterday - today, you wouldn't catch me out there wrapped in my overcoat and scarf. Talk about summer to winter... isn't there a season missing this year? Anyway, you come in, its good to see you. I know you've not been able to come round these past few weeks. I've missed you. It's not the same taking a G&T on your own. I do try, to keep my spirits up; but of course it has to be just a G!

So, how have you occupied yourself since last we met? You cram a lot in, you do. Not like me, I'm getting so slow. It took me all morning to clear the broad bean stalks and barrow them to the compost heap. Mind you, we had a good crop this year. And you appreciate my beans, don't you. If it wasn't getting dark I'd show you the runners, still producing, what a season. Prolific year - that's a good word, prolific, abundant, loads of beans... Like you, full of beans!! You come and tell me your news, that's it, coat on the back of the kitchen chair and come through to the sitting room, yes, I'll be there in my own time, you make yourself comfy. I'll bring yours through.

Oof, I sometimes think when I plonk myself down in this old sofa, I'll never manage to get back up. You've chosen today's book then, that's one of my favourites too. I like stories about mischievous children. They remind me of my more youthful times, and of course having you round here too.

Come on then, story time with Grandpa then our G&T. You can't beat a good session of Grin and Tickle with your wriggly, giggly grandson every so often can you!

Steve Redshaw

November 16

The Lucky-Lucky Day

"Consider the daffodil. And while you're doing that, I'll be over here, looking through your stuff." Jack Handey.

The Lucky-Lucky Man had an amazing memory which was essential in his profession. He remembered the number 88 bus went past the police station. This might not have been a problem if it kept going. He knew it was time to carry the rucksack over the Uplands. He marched through a snicket and a small cul-de-sac. Then over a gate like a gymnast, still carrying the eleven kg pack. He saw a small seventies style house near some trees. It was his Auntie Gladys and Uncle Harvey's detached hideaway. Down the rough track he soon reached the door.

He knocked on the window even though there was a perfectly good working doorbell.

A cheerful woman in her eighties opened the door. "Norman", she explained gleefully, although that is not the Lucky-Lucky man's real name. "Come in and put your rucksack down. Have a cup of tea, just made one. Are you looking forward to the Jubilee, Norman? Everyone looking at the same thing. What a great sense of community! Here's your Uncle Harvey now."

"Colin, how are you, Mr Moneybags, and what's in the rucksack?"

"Business, my business. Christmas stock."

"In June?"

Nobody gave it a thought how he was known by two different names to Auntie Gladys and Uncle Harvey. It's only to be expected for a man with six birth certificates. It also helped him to improve that memory: which acquaintance knew which name or nickname and yes, Nick was one of the names.

Auntie Gladys offered Norman the compulsory customary cup of tea that working class hospitality always demanded. Discussion turned to the imminent jubilee and monarchy; the Lucky-Lucky man was a big fan of the Royal Family but not quite for the same reasons as Auntie Gladys and Uncle Harvey.

"If they're looking at the Queen and not looking at me, if they are in her business, they're not in mine," thought Colin/Norman/Nick.

Unusually the TV on and was tuned to the ITV coverage of the Jubilee; a vox pop of opinions. The great unwashed seemed to give a unanimous thumbs up to the Queen and her firm.

"Colin, do you remember the load of money raised by our Silver Jubilee charity Corgis Assist Single Homeless: C.A.S.H. I can't believe we made two grand! Or the Punk rock t-shirts showing a depressed corgi with a safety pin through his nose."

"It was murder getting the dog to wear the safety pin for the photo."

"Norman. Do you remember just before the coronation and the Vicarage had been burgled and fifty coronation bibles being swiped? All of a sudden, your Dad had plenty of money and a new TV set. I had a new gas cooker and four bibles which I was able to take to the Hucknall Sunday school and sell."

Colin was enjoying the sit down. But the rest of his journey loomed, and the rucksack contents were heavy.

On screen, a distinctly shifty-looking Prince Andrew accompanied the Queen down a short flight of steps. "Just like Cousin Martin before the court case," they laughed.

"Colin, do you remember when I told you what a Jubilee really meant the day when all debts got cancelled?"

"Yeah, uncle you already 'splained that to death."

"Norman, your Mom met your dad in court."

He knew it was time to go when the good old days stories were coming out.

"Your mum wasn't like us. She was born into money and then she met your dad and got fond of the bad boys..." He saw himself out. This was embarrassing.

A short hike to the big wall he knew well. The Lucky-Lucky man stevedored the heavy rucksack over the seven foot wall of the children's home and got his breath back with some effort.

"Happy Jubbly, kids, and Santa has all the receipts."

Chris Wright

November 17

The Telling Thump Of It

I was woken by the postman this morning. Not personally, but by a dull thump as something heavy landed on the hall mat. Now what could that be, I wondered. A telephone directory? Or a clothes catalogue? A telephone directory wouldn't go through the letterbox, and I don't buy clothes from catalogues. Sadly, I knew by the telling thump of it what it was. I closed my eyes and took a deep breath to prepare myself for the standard rejection letter that always began with; "Thank you for your recent letter," which, in the case of a writer, is not only a letter but the first three chapters of a novel which can be anywhere between fifty and seventy pages, and a synopsis of the story.

From the top of the stairs, I could see it was indeed an A4 envelope. Not any old A4 envelope – but a heavy duty, expandable, light manila, self-seal A4 envelope. The type of envelope that you can only afford to buy two of at any time. One to send your dreams off, and one to bring them back, as nightmares, if you're not lucky.

After two cups of morning kick-me-up, strong enough to put a zing into a rhinoceros, I opened the envelope and took out its contents. I read the apology for responding with a standard letter - which was par for the course, as was the excuse: "We have a small client base and are not currently taking on new authors." I Googled the company before I wrote to them. Their client base was anything but small. But I digress. The third paragraph said, "If you would like our book on the correct way to present your work to a literary agent, please send a cheque and self-addressed envelope to... etc., etc." The cheek of it. The book on how to present your work to a literary agent was the most thumbed book on my bookcase - and had been for five years. I thought about writing and telling them, but I could see that the book suggestion was also standard. The standard letter ended with a standard phrase: "Good luck finding an agent."

Oh, well, to wish someone good luck in their endeavours was better than wishing them bad luck – even if it was standard. But enough of my cynicism. If anyone reads this short story, please know that after I had written it, after I had vented my anger in words, which is the best way to vent anger - the pen is mightier and all that - my disappointment waned, until I checked the name of the agent on my submissions list and found that I had written to the company in August 2011 and it was now January 2012.

    +   +

More determined than ever to get my novel out into the world, I thought, to hell with buying two more heavy-duty, expandable, light manila, self-seal A4 envelopes - and I self-published.

Sincere good luck to whoever reads this story. May your dreams come true.

Madalyn Morgan

November 18

Garry And Barry Meet A Celebrity

"Do you still love me, Harriet?

"Cat print. Harriet. I'll change when we get there. No one expects me in cats, ones that stare back. I'm supposed to be the quintessential dog person... Psychology you see.

"We shall be incredibly early at this rate... Excellent. Black shoes. Thank you."

+ +

The shadow of the bridge too large, tunnel too small, concealed the men, even in their so-called high-vis, in the all-orange uniform.

"Trousers too," Garry moaned, "we look like Guantanamo rejects."

"The Queen's train will be here in a few hours," Barry stated matter-of-factly. "These rails won't check themselves."

The region's top team were now reduced to track checking after the 'cheese on the line' incident. They walked with the speed of death row inmates. Garry was in lecture mode.

"Why do we even need a queen anyway?"

"President?"

"Nothing. Just witans, local councils like in Saxon times."

"They had King Alfred."

The two troublemakers strolled toward the centre of the short tunnel. In the orange overalls, looking like dads doing their kids' community service. They carried on checking every sleeper and rail in the conscientious way you do when so bored you actually do the work to pass the time.

"Five to twelve, Barry. Are you sure they got the right message this time?"

"They betta, or lose £200 a week of my custom," Barry threatened

Walking in further, it was clear the tunnel consisted of two large road bridges with a three-metre gap.

"I told them to do it opposite the pub, the Red Lion!"

"There are two Red Lions in Nanton, Baz!!"

"I told them the one on the Breedham Road."

"Should be OK, I s'pose," Garry reassured a little.

Suddenly a voice from ten metres above. "Anyone there?"

"Yeah! Delivery for Barry Stains again. Mr Stains: keep clear!" The guys moved exactly not at all.

A Deliveroo bag bungee-ed down to within 50 cm of Garry's head.

"Missed me," he shouted and grabbed the padded pack.

"Can we have our bag back?"

"Come and get it!" taunted Garry, extracting his salad and passing the inner brown wrapped rugby ball to Barry.

"Don't forget me chips, Gaz," insisted Barry and his mate passed over the red packs.

"I'll bring the bag on Friday! Don't let the coppers get you on that dual carriageway either!"

A grumble from above then silence. The workers settled down to a troglodytic picnic with their toolboxes for stools.

"What are those initials for, BSS, Barry Stephen Stains?"

"No."

"Simon? Stan? Shaun? Shitty? Shitty Stains. Ha ha ha."

"No, and piss off, Gaz. You'd just take the piss."

They ate in silence for a few minutes punctuated with the occasional "Selwyn" or "Shadwell" or "St John".

"Side, Baz!" Garry shouted even though Barry was just a metre away. A train was coming. They expected to see commuters staring as usual; the train flowing at a carefully steady pace. At this point Barry realised he had no hands free and wolfed all the French fries in the pack in one go; rendered mute, he nodded at Garry and they grabbed all the kit.

Just one unit and two carriages in the train, very odd. Odder, it was stopping.

Under the dim work lights, there was an electric window opening, also very odd. In her off-duty cat-blouse, the Queen of England stared directly at Barry.

"Excuse me. Would you mind telling me where we are, please?"

Barry was trying to say, "Just a mile outside Nanton, your majesty." What came out was closer to:-

"thssh o mnul Ofthul nntn url nfchstr."

Particles of chip and possibly chicken and bacon wrap reached the monarch, a couple reminded Garry of tears on the cat's eye of the revolting print.

Garry started to belly laugh which his age could have been lethal. The window rolled up smoothly with Mrs Windsor maintaining some dignity.

Collapsed against the wall of the bridge, Garry was just getting his breath back.

"Saville." My middle name is Saville."

Garry laughed so much he nearly lost his cheeseburger too.

Chris Wright

November 19

Once Upon A Time

Once upon a time and then thrunce upon a brime a grangely gligh was hunning his fradely lide glumpily along a prondace grice, when tumpily he shad a fremdice. Spadish it was and so swentingly praneful that hadenly he was ortruned and engerwalded. 'Rastucks, praine fremdice, rastux,' he chenged. 'Weng dreck, nur.'

'Nastwerds' it respraiged and glentilly extrangelled him. 'Venglecks,' and the fremdice then sworbed and prewicksally frinded. The gligh gid a yube; he braunched to renchal with a smooding medge. He swenged yarpelly in a slenching clube, with hernchal nuntode, for the fremdice was tung dasstile blad and smulled with flissom mertade, so that he was gransingly daunceful.

He grumped he was outgrooned and engerwelded but raidily he slod and restenged his migful graut – slumbily and prossedly until hundilly he broze.

'Twen reng I' he scompted, 'Twen?'

'Ninshanks! Noss. Turays I froime. I'll grent my sploutly treng and unenttwers shall I obraze. Drentilly will I be swenged. I'll exen braze till pinwends. This I frume, grenfullest of fremdices. Altay, altay, till twunce upon a nime, altay.'

Chris Rowe

November 20

Bolero

"A friend and I are going to a concert in the Albert Hall. Would you like to come?"

A concert? Like the ones in the social hall where Dad works? With a dance afterwards?

And he's invited me. To a concert in London. We're to go in his friend's car, not by train.

"'Yes, please."

The Edgware Road is busy. Neil chews his fingers, but we arrive in time, go up the steps and into the hall. It's vast! We go upstairs, find our seats.

There is a hum of chatter, the rustle of programmes, an air of expectation. I am impressed, peering over the heads to look down on the stage with its rows of chairs.

The hubbub stops. Onto the stage come the members of the orchestra. They take their seats. The conductor arrives to resounding applause. He bows and takes up his position on the little platform. I expect the lights to go out, like they do in the Borough Hall when the play starts. Some people in the audience have music scores. Perhaps it is so they can read them.

The conductor raises his baton. A hush, a stillness as he waits for silence. Then a quiet de-de-de-dum, repeated over and over again by just one drummer. My heart stops.

One by one more instruments join in, the same rhythm on and on, and now my heart is beating with it. I'm on the edge of my seat, leaning forward, carried away with the increasing tension, the primeval beat as the piece comes to a crescendo. I don't want it to stop, but it does with a flourish and I'm clapping until my palms hurt.

On the way home, I am replaying it all in my head, in my chest, my heart beating to the throb. It never went away. I can hear it now as I travel back to when I was seventeen, going to my first concert with my first boyfriend to hear Ravel's *Bolero* in The Royal Albert Hall.

Wendy Goulstone

November 21

Devil Women

The tiny square of asphalt was tucked away behind the village hall and surrounded by long grass. It served no discernible purpose. It could have been intended as a base for a shed or a coal bunker or perhaps it was somewhere to put the dustbin. The village children knew what it was really for. It was a place for them to play out of sight of any passing adult who might interfere with their games.

Sean had just finished drawing the diagram when the first large raindrops splashed down.

'Bother,' he said, looking up at the charcoal grey clouds. 'Go away.'

It began to rain harder, obliterating the chalk marks that he had carefully drawn.

'I'm getting wet,' Gemma whined.

'It's not my fault,' Sean said, scowling. 'We'll have to go inside and try again. The village hall's open. It's library afternoon.'

He shoved the chalk and the book into his anorak pocket and headed for the back door of the hall. The other children followed. Mrs. Turner was just packing away the library books.

'Sean Jackson, what are you and your little band of hooligans doing in here?'

'We're just looking for somewhere out of the rain, Mrs. Turner. We won't be a nuisance, honest.'

Sean looked at her with his little lost puppy expression that always appealed to ladies of a certain age. Mrs. Turner had a soft spot for Sean. True, he was a bit of a rogue, but he did have those big blue eyes and those cute freckles on his nose and he was always very polite.

'Very well,' she agreed. 'I'll be back in half an hour to lock up, so make sure you don't make a mess.'

She put on her hat and coat, picked up her handbag and set off for the Rose and Crown. Everyone knew that she always called in on

Fridays for a couple of drinks and the latest village gossip with Mrs. Carter the landlady. As the pub was closed in the afternoons, they could slander the entire population of the village in complete privacy, without any fear of retribution.

'She'll be at least an hour,' Sean said. 'Let's get started.'

He took the chalk out of his pocket and started to draw on the bare wooden floorboards just behind the billiard table, where he would be hidden from view by its floor length dust cover. The others watched him carefully, memorising every line and letter as he meticulously completed the diagram.

'Right then,' he said. 'Katie, have you got the candles?'

Katie pulled five dark blue candles out of her coat pocket. One of them was a bit bent.

'They're supposed to be black,' Sean said.

Katie shrugged. 'My parents didn't have any black ones, only these.'

'I suppose they'll have to do.' Sean sighed theatrically. 'Put them there in the points.' He indicated the five points of the pentagram. 'Who's got the matches?'

Colin put his hand up. 'I have.'

'You're not in school now,' Sean said.

Colin blushed and threw the matches to Katie. She lit the five navy blue candles. Gemma produced a bundle of joss sticks and stuffed them in a jam jar for Katie to light. A cloud of sweet smelling smoke billowed across the billiard table, setting off the smoke alarm. Colin quickly opened the window and started flapping at the smoke with his blazer. The candles went out.

Katie picked up the jam jar of joss sticks and ran into the ladies' cloakroom. She tipped the smouldering sticks into the sink and turned on the taps. The joss sticks fizzled out and she shoved the whole soggy mess into the incinerator. She rinsed out the jam jar and left it under the sink.

Sean grabbed a chair from the stack by the door and climbed onto it. He tried to reach the smoke detector, but he wasn't quite tall enough.

'If you don't turn it off pretty quick, somebody'll hear it,' Katie pointed out as it beeped frantically.

'All right then, smart arse, you turn it off!' Sean snapped at her.

With a complacent expression on her face, Katie took one of the cues from the rack next to the billiard table, sauntered slowly across the hall and prodded at the smoke alarm's plastic casing until she succeeded in silencing it. She replaced the cue in the rack and waited for Sean to say something.

Sean put the chair back on the stack, making a lot of noise. He took a torch out of his pocket, switched off the hall lights and began to issue orders. Katie smirked at him.

'Colin, shut that window. Gemma and Matthew, close the curtains. Katie, don't bother re-lighting the candles. We can use my torch. Now, everybody get inside the pentagram.'

Katie was full of herself now and challenged Sean again.

'What, all of us? In that little space? Shouldn't there be thirteen of us for a real coven? Not just five?'

Matthew, Gemma's little brother, had been keeping very quiet in case the others noticed him and sent him home. That was what usually happened just as things were getting interesting.

He said, 'Of course we can all fit in if we stand very close together and don't move about too much.'

'Go home, Matthew,' Gemma said automatically.

'No, he can stay,' Sean said. 'Mind you don't smudge any of the lines. It could be dangerous.' The five of them stepped into the pentagram, Katie lifting her feet high.

'Don't we need a sacrifice? Does anyone have a black cockerel or a goat?' she asked.

Matthew was shocked. 'You're not really going to kill a goat, are you?'

'No, of course not, stupid. This isn't voodoo,' Sean snapped. He glared at Katie. 'We're going to chant in Latin, backwards. Here.'

He handed each of them a photocopy of some Latin verse. It was a translation of *Twinkle, Twinkle Little Star* that his older brother had done for homework last term, but the others wouldn't know that.

'On the count of three. One, two, three.'

They began to chant, very quietly at first, stumbling over the words, and then louder as their confidence grew. The flickering torch light made the familiar surroundings of the village hall turn into something creepy and frightening. The stack of chairs became a crouching monster lurking in the corner. The snooker cues were tall, bony creatures about to attack. At the other end of the hall the library cases were full of menace. Anything could be locked inside them, just waiting to be released. Even the lights over the billiard table looked like strange flying things hanging in mid-air.

They came to the end of the verse. Silence. Gemma thought the dust cover was moving, but she was too scared to say so. Sean was about to say, 'Again,' when a sharp click cut across the silence.

The door at the far end of the hall opened. Sean switched off his torch. A shaft of light illuminated a dark figure standing in the doorway.

Gemma gasped, 'It's the Devil, it's the Devil.' She buried her head in her hands.

Sean grabbed Gemma's hand and held it tight. He hadn't believed anything would really happen. His heart was beating faster and he couldn't breathe. Matthew hid under his coat. Next time he wanted to be sent home. Colin was so frightened he couldn't move and stayed frozen to the spot, still in the middle of the pentagram. Katie crept behind the others so that they were between her and whatever it was. She didn't really believe it was the Devil, but you couldn't be too careful.

There were other figures barely visible in the gloom, all moving towards the billiard table. Someone or something sniffed and then sneezed violently.

'What's that smell? Is something burning?'

'Why is it so dark in here?' another voice said.

The lights snapped on. The five children quickly wriggled under the billiard table so that they were hidden by the dustcover. In front of them were a dozen of the village ladies, all dressed in leotards. Mrs. Durrant, the vicar's wife, turned on the cassette player and loud music boomed out.

'It's my mum,' Colin hissed. 'We've got to get out of here.'

Sean grabbed Colin to stop him from running away. 'Not until we've cleaned this lot up, you don't.'

They frantically rubbed out the chalk marks, using Gemma's clean hankie and Sean's Manchester United scarf. Katie gathered up her candles. The pounding music covered any noise they were making as the ladies bounced up and down like a team of demented, land-bound synchronised swimmers in response to Mrs. Durrant's shouted commands.

'Grapevine to the left, ladies. Keep those arms going.'

Slowly and carefully the children crept out from under the billiard table and crawled along the side of the hall to the back door. Luckily the ladies were far too engrossed in their aerobics routine to notice them.

+   +

Many years later, after Sean and Gemma were married, Gemma told the story to one of her friends.

'We were so scared,' she said. 'We really thought we'd conjured up something horrid. But there were no demons, just a bunch of over-weight middle-aged women doing aerobics to *Devil Woman* by Cliff Richard. And every time I hear that song I can smell those joss sticks.'

Fran Neatherway

November 22

Seeing Stars

"I'm not watching any more flippin' soap operas," growled Peggy, leafing through the *Radio Times*.

Derek looked up, remote control in hand. Where had this come from?

"But what about the Dingles? I can't just abandon them."

"I couldn't care less about the Dingles or anyone else from *Emmerdale*. It's fantasy. Life isn't like that. It's not real."

Peggy shifted position. Now to deliver the killer blow.

"There are some lectures on BBC4 about science. I'd like to educate myself. You could do with a bit of that as well." She enjoyed that last line in particular.

Derek's face crimsoned, almost to a gammon hue. How dare she deprive him of his lifeblood? How could he exist without his soaps?

Peggy and Derek had been together nearly twenty years but recently things had become a little tetchy. He'd been picked up for not using all of the toothpaste in the tube, not leaving the hand towels in a perfectly horizontal position, and for wearing socks for more than a week in a row. The writing was on the wall.

Not just that. He'd noticed Peggy deep in conversation with 'hot' Rod from next door – he of the flaming sideburns and the classic Ford Capri. They'd been talking about satellites, and shooting stars. Rod had a telescope and was always at his bedroom window.

"I'm going to the spare room," said Derek defiantly, "and watch what I want."

"Go then," said Peggy, decisively, switching channels.

For Peggy and Derek, this wasn't the end of the beginning.

More like the beginning of the end.

John Howes

November 23

The Three Brothers

Once upon a time there were three brothers, Gerald, Dan and Will. Gerald was Something Big in the City. Dan owned property in Brixton, and Will had just finished a Medieval Media Studies course at university. When he saw how rich his brothers were, Will decided to go to the City to seek his fortune. He packed a sleeping bag and his money in his rucksack, put some bars of chocolate into his pocket and set off for the railway station. The train was very crowded, but Will managed to find a seat, when a little old lady, dressed in rags, squeezed her way through the crush. Will jumped to his feet, and gave her his seat and a bar of chocolate.

'Thank you, my dear,' she said in a soft voice. 'You are most kind, and your goodness will not go unrewarded.'

The train pulled into Euston Station. Will turned to say goodbye but the little old lady had disappeared. And so had his rucksack. Will decided to find Gerald, who would surely welcome him into his home in Bloomsbury. He rang the bell and heard the clip-clop of high-heeled shoes. The door opened and an elegant young lady stood before him.

'What do you want?' she snapped in a cold, high-pitched voice..

'I've come to stay with my brother,' said Will. 'Is he in?'

'Wait there, he's busy,' she said, and shut the door.

The minutes passed. At last Gerald opened the door with an abrupt, "What are you doing here?"

'I've come to make my fortune,' said Will. 'Please, may I stay here with you?'

'You've got a cheek,' snarled Gerald. 'I don't want you around when I am entertaining important contacts. So clear off.'

So Will set off to find Dan, who would surely welcome him into his home in Chelsea. He click-clacked the iron knocker, and the door opened to reveal a woman with bleached hair, an enormous bosom and a very short skirt.

'What do you want?' she drawled.

'I've come to stay with my brother, Dan,' said Will. 'Is he in?'

'He's gone to see his tenants,' she said. 'Come in. Make yourself cosy on the sofa.'

Will glanced round at the cheap prints on the walls, depicting women in various stages of undress.

'Lovely, ain't they?' she leered in his ear. 'What's a nice young lad like you doing in London?'

She pursed her lips to meet his.

'Get out! Now!' Dan stood in the doorway, dripping with gold jewellery, his beer-belly hanging over his belt.

'I said, get out! What you waiting for?'

'I've come to make my fortune,' said Will, 'but my rucksack has been stolen and I have no money. Please may I stay here with you?'

'Are you deaf or what?' roared Dan, and frog-marched him to the door and pushed him down the steps.

It was getting dark and beginning to rain.

'I'll have to find a corner to sleep in,' thought Will, as he passed several people huddled in doorways, hands reaching out.

'Sorry, mate, I'm destitute myself. Have a bar of chocolate. Do you know of anywhere I could sleep?'

'Try Battersea Bridge, that's if you don't get beaten up by the regulars.'

So Will made his way to Battersea Bridge, and sure enough he was met with hostile stares and threats.

'Sorry to disturb you, mates,' he said, and shared his last bar of chocolate.

He was just turning away when he heard a soft voice saying, 'There's a space by me, my dear. You can come and keep warm by me.'

And there was the little old lady. Will greeted her warmly and kissed her on the cheek. All that night they lay close together, shielding each other from the cold breeze. Will woke next morning to find that the little old lady had disappeared, but in her place lay the most beautiful girl he had ever seen, her long hair touching his cheek. And there, too, was his rucksack, with all his belongings inside it, and a big bag of buns to share with his new friends.

Wendy Goulstone

November 24

Flying

To make life interesting, my partner in the aircraft was a rather cavalier pilot called Gary whose idea of a preflight check, on finding a mystery bolt, was inclined to chuck it over the hedge and carry on.

Off we went and climbed to 2,000 feet. It was shocking to look down at the smog we exist in as the air became clear and fresh. The green fields of our homeland stretched out before us with a spaghetti of tiny roads taking others on their journeys to mysterious places. Brown muddy canals gleamed silver or gold in the morning sun as they, with rivers and brooks meandered hither and thither, stitching together the patchwork of fields and woods with black, gold and silver threads.

In the clear air I felt sure I could smell fuel. On landing, the smell of fuel was even stronger and an inspection showed it running from the tank under our feet. A helpful chap with a car was dispatched to buy some more fuel and find a motorist shop to purchase a product optimistically called *Stop Leak*. I was feeling distinctly uneasy about this cunning plan.

On return to the field, the product seemed to have done its job. We bid goodbye to our fellow aviators. Half way back, the dreaded smell returned with fuel running over the floor. Scenarios of a fire or an explosion crossed my mind. What would I do? Stay with the machine and burn to death or abandon it and jump out? After a tense conference with pilot Gary, we decided to continue and attempt to get back to base. The engine was beginning to protest in a very unpleasant way. Then it all went quiet in the engine room and we were now a glider using gravity as a fuel to get us back. On landing, the Red Kites grudgingly moved out of the way, no doubt thinking, "Bloody amateurs."

I have never been so pleased to feel the tyres kiss Mother Earth. My flying buddy died some years later of natural causes at a good old age, much to my surprise.

Patrick Garrett

November 25

A Village Evening

An extract from my diary, 1960

I need my mum to order me two young farmers' booklets for me. There is so much I need to learn about farming. I will offer to send a postal order to pay for them. I want number seven, *Implements and Farm Machinery*. Also I will remind her I need more socks, else I might be working in bare feet. This diary is about a month behind due to milking and hay making plus rehearsals for the play, now that I have joined Young Farmers and volunteered. I am in the chorus but I do have a solo.

I am going to write about the last performance. I am writing this on Sunday morning. I dragged myself out of bed at 10 am and had some breakfast. My head is so full with the play and everything we were doing at Holsworthy Village Hall. It holds 300 people and was packed with some standing at the back too. I started to feel miserable and sad but it was so exciting that I soon forgot.

I had been given the morning off - no milking today. I just got ready and picked up my bike and cycled the five miles to Bradworthy, parked my bike by the garage and got picked up to be driven the eight miles to Holsworthy. I will keep my programme and newspaper cutting in my journal too.

At the end of the performance, Ivor the director made a speech and then drew the raffle, a box of chocs and 50 cigarettes. Then we did one last chorus and scooted off to get changed. The man who had won the chocolates sent them backstage for me, for singing so beautifully he said. I was thrilled.

Then a man brought in a tray filled with glasses of champagne and sherries. We had a drink and Ivor played his organ and the company entertained us. Ivor got out his community song book and, after some more champagne, we got stuck into singing. I did *Ilkley Moor* for them. I was the only one who could do the accent. I think I sing better with alcohol. Then we had some sherry. At 12 o'clock we sang some hymns and, spiritless at 12.30 am, we hurriedly packed up and everyone went round kissing. I'm glad the lights were low to hide my blushes. Then we all piled into Ivor's old croc and I was dropped off at Bradworthy where I claimed my bike and cycled back to our farm.

Oh it was a wonderful experience. I shall never forget it. I seem able to cope with the alcohol. I cycled home safely at 1 o'clock and went to bed quietly by candlelight.

Ruth Hughes

November 26

The Chair

The house was going cheap, so cheap that we could pay outright.

'The owners are going abroad', he said. 'They want a quick sale.'

So, we had a quick look around, paid the deposit, signed the documents and moved in with mops and buckets, and the minimum of furniture, to transform this neglected building into a home.

'It will look great when we've decorated throughout, installed new carpets, a new kitchen and bathroom.'

But we had little in the bank now, and most of our dreams would have to wait. In the sitting room the previous owners had left a chair. Gerald scrubbed it, polished it and it looked quite respectable. But, it was odd, there was something odd about it. If I sat on it, I had the feeling that it resented my presence.

I did not mention this to Gerald.

'Just nonsense,' he would say. 'Just your imagination running wild.' But it happened every time, until I stopped sitting on the chair altogether and put it in the spare bedroom. Next morning it was back in the sitting room.

'Why did you move the chair?' he asked, a hint of annoyance creeping in.

'I don't like it. It doesn't fit in with our other furniture.'

'Well, that's great after all the time I spent cleaning it up, sanding it, polishing it, when there are plenty of other jobs I could have been doing. And I like it. So it stays in here, where it belongs.'

It was no good arguing with him. He always had the last word. Ever since we moved into this house he had always won any disagreement, always made the decisions, chosen the colour schemes, the furniture, even decided what we had for dinner. The loving, considerate man I had married had been transformed into a dictatorial controller.

So the chair stayed in the same spot in the room where we had first seen it, a dark corner where the sun never reached. I avoided it, never dusted it, never looked at it, but I felt its brooding presence so strongly that I began to spend my evenings alone in the dining room.

Gerald said nothing. It was if he was glad to avoid my company, to be rid of me. Some days he spoke only when necessary. There was no rapport between us. He began to go out in the evenings, returning late at night, long after I had gone to bed.

One evening, when he was out, I went into the sitting room to retrieve a book I had left in there. The chair was in the centre of the room, facing me, with a presence as if someone was sitting in it, staring at me. I edged round it, sidling round the furniture, but I could feel its eyes following me.

Its eyes? Why did I say its eyes?

I found my book and slipped warily behind the sofa, but it was still watching me, drawing me towards it like a magnetic force, impelling me to sit on it. On an impulse, I seized it up, my hands so hot they seemed to be burning, and threw it out into the yard. I went into the kitchen, found the meat cleaver and went outside. I smashed and smashed in a frenzy, swinging the cleaver wildly.

'What do you think you are doing?' His angry voice in my ear startled me.

In mid-swipe the cleaver swung down. He fell to the ground, blood gushing from his head, onto the shattered splinters of the chair.

Wendy Goulstone

November 27

A Room With A View

As I entered the room my heart was pounding. I was one of only a handful of people that Zack had invited from the office. Tonight had to be the night.

I scanned the room and spotted him, looking exceptionally handsome.

I worked my way through the partying crowd and headed over to him near the bar.

'Happy birthday!' I said.

'Sarah, you came!' he said, seeming delighted to see me.

'I got you a present,' I said, not able to stop my nervous smile.

'You shouldn't have,' he said, placing down his pint to take the gift.

He tore off the paper and his face started to glow. Just as I hoped it would.

'This is a first edition?' he said with awe, flicking through the book.

I nodded.

'How did you know?' he asked.

I shrugged. He'd only told me in passing once that his favourite novel was *A Room With a View*. It reminded him of his late mother, and it was reading it with her that had made him fall in love with literature. I remembered because when you're in love, you take notice.

I was just about to say that - the very words I'd practised – when Zack called over someone to join us. 'Look, Lizzy. Look what Sarah got me.' A gorgeous, stick thin woman grabbed the book.

'A smelly old book,' she giggled. 'How nice.'

'It's a first edition.' He looked at me. 'This must have cost a fortune.'

'You're only thirty once,' I stuttered.

'Sorry, this is Lizzy,' he said. 'My girlfriend.'

The world stopped turning.

'Girlfriend?'

'Yes. Oh, thanks for this,' he said, kissing me on the cheek.

As he started to show everyone around him the book and how I saw that not one other person understood the importance, my heart cracked in two.

I stepped away, unable to bear the pain. I knew then and there, my heart would never be whole again.

Lindsay Woodward

November 28

Salad Dodger

Of my first school, in Sutton Bridge, I have little memory other than its general location. We would walk up to the main road – without having to cross it – past tonsured Lennie Laytus's shop where you could get anything from gobstoppers to a haircut, towards the Bridge then down another side road. In a hall just before turning right to school I saw water turned to wine. The goal was no doubt religious instruction or reinforcement. Curious the mindset that would see this fostered by reducing the miracle at Cana to a parlour trick.

The headmistress shared my surname without being related to Grandad Bailey. Mum had provided a note to say that I didn't like salad (the child is father to the man) and should not be made to eat it.

'Your mum's far too faddy', Mrs Bailey grumbled as she swept the offending item – a shred of lettuce, a slice of tomato? – onto the plate of fat Brian, sitting beside me on the bench at dinner-time. That was the only occasion I remember the matter coming up; perhaps the head was standing in for someone more attuned to spoilt bastard's special dietary requirements. When I relayed her comment, maybe not so innocently, to Mum, she was all for going to the school to have it out with her namesake. That didn't happen. I ate no item of salad before reaching the age of majority.

Walking to school aged four or five, being entrusted with notes for other kids' parents, these are relics of a time when children were viewed far more as small adults than princes and princesses to be indulged and obeyed without question by their parent or parents. It was strictly against my orders that, she admitted years later, Mum had followed me and my friends to school at a discreet distance on my first day and perhaps a few after that. I can't see me leaving infant school nowadays at Christmas, laden with balloons and party trinkets, to get into a car with a man never seen near the place before. Quite right too, but quite

209

right then also. The driver was Uncle Ted, on home leave from the army.

David G Bailey

November 29

Lucky

The sun was breaking through the clouds as the bus inched slowly forwards. Margo stared out of the window at the people hurrying past, most with their heads down as they rushed hastily towards the shops and offices where they would be confined for the next eight hours or so as life passed them by. She wondered how many of them had hidden health issues. Maybe they wouldn't find out until it was too late. She supposed she was fortunate in that respect.

Taking a mirror from her bag, she studied her face. There were a few crow's feet around her eyes, a tangle of faint thread veins on a cheek but no signs of any potential problems. She'd thought her headaches and dizzy flutterings were just part of who she was; she'd always been a nervous type. It was Jeannie who made her go to see Dr. Martin, insisting she couldn't go off and enjoy her travels if she was worrying about Margo back at home. She checked her watch, realising that even though she'd managed to get the first appointment of the day, she was still going to be very late. Maura would be spitting feathers. She leant back and tried to focus on her breathing and being in the present moment like Dr. Martin had advised.

'How were things at home these days?' he'd asked.

'Oh, you know,' she'd replied, trying to sound flippant, 'same old...'

His kind eyes had searched unsuccessfully for hers before he'd asked how Jim was.

'You know Jim,' she'd answered, forcing a tight smile.

'Yes,' he'd agreed, more firmly now; he did indeed know Jim.

He had held the prescription suspended between them for a few interminable seconds before telling her to come back in a couple of weeks and reiterating that she knew where they were if she needed anything.

+   +

Jim belched loudly and threw the empty can at the bin, smirking as it bounced off and spun to a stop on the rug. Margo could clear that up later. It would give her something useful to do after a day gossiping at her so called bloody work with that snooty mate of hers. Wiping his mouth with the back of his sleeve he unfolded the letter that had come that morning, glaring at it from under tightly knotted brows. Bloody nerve. What right did they think they had to stop his benefits.

'*Higher sanction...*' he read, '...*failure to take a job that your work coach has told you about.*'

Who the hell did they think they were? There was no way he was going into any warehouse full of bloody immigrants and the like. Buggers coming over here, taking all the jobs while genuine people like him were penalised. Damn the lot of them to hell.

He picked up another can from the floor, worrying at the ring pull with his thumb. How the hell would he manage? Margo would have to pull her bloody finger out for a start, get a few more shifts in. Lazy cow.

Screwing the letter into a tight ball, he launched it at a vase of daffodils on the windowsill. He'd soon put a stop to her wasting money on poxy flowers. She could pack in catching the bus too. A decent walk would do her good; she could do with losing a bit. He smiled smugly to himself. There's an answer to everything if you're clever enough to find it. God he was good. Too bloody smart to do some dead end job with a load of weirdos who couldn't even speak the lingo. He gave the ring pull a sharp tug and took a long satisfied swig.

+ +

Margo's fingers tapped nervously on the pole as she stood and waited for the bus to stop. Maura was bound to make her work back her time owing today and she'd been in such a rush this morning she'd forgotten to prepare dinner before she left home. Jim would be hungry and a hungry Jim was an angry Jim. She didn't know what she could do though.

A sudden jolt and hiss of brakes propelled her backwards onto an empty seat. Rising quickly, she looked down at a crumpled copy of the latest *Racing Post* bearing the shape of her bottom. Claiming it quickly, she sent out grateful thanks to its careless owner for sparing her the aggravation of also having forgotten Jim's paper, while saving her money to boot. Maybe, along with the money saved from the lifts home Jeannie had been giving her, she might be able to scrape together enough for fish and chips later. Perhaps today wouldn't be so bad after all, and she was looking forward to seeing Jeannie at lunch time and catching up with her travel plans. Lucky devil. Pushing the newspaper into her bag Margo hurried off the bus.

+   +

Jim patted his rumbling stomach and lumbered to the kitchen. She'd better have left him something decent today; yesterday's macaroni cheese was bloody disgusting.

Inspecting the contents of the neatly packed lunchbox, he sneered at the cheese and pickle sandwiches. What was it with Margo and cheese? Slimy, bland, and tasteless, just like bloody Margo. He snorted at his humour. No imagination, that was her trouble. When he cut her housekeeping, she'd have to put a bit more thought into things. Useless cow. He was starving. He'd call into the Crown, have a pie and a pint, and do a bit of networking before going to the bookies.

He pulled on his jacket. Despite that bloody letter, he was feeling lucky. A nice little win was long overdue and he had a sure thing for the 3.15. What did they say – God takes away with one hand and gives back with the other or some crap like that. Not that he'd be sharing with Margo if he won. It wouldn't do for her to think he had a bob or two. No, if he won he would spend it wisely. On himself. Whistling happily, he set off down the road.

+   +

Jeannie flung her bag on the floor and flopped onto a chair.

'That Maura's a bloomin' slave driver. I'm not going to miss her miserable mug one little bit.' She leant towards Margo, 'How did you get on at the docs?'

'He said my blood pressure's through the roof.' Margo shrugged, 'It explains the headaches I suppose. He's given me some tablets and said I've got to try to eliminate any stress in my life.'

'Good luck with that! You'll need to get rid of that useless lump at home first.' As Margo's eyes began to water, she hugged her tightly. 'Guess what, I booked my plane ticket yesterday. No, don't look like that. There were a couple of seats free next to mine. I reckon one of them could have your name on. What do you say?'

'I wish! I struggle to find the fare to work, never mind round the world.'

'I'm worried about going away and leaving you though. I can't believe that in this day and age you haven't even got a bank card. Why do you let him bully you like that?'

'I'll be ok Jeannie.' Margo tried to sound convincing. 'I wouldn't know where to start with a bank card. If I know what's in my purse I can manage it,' she recited, forcing a smile. 'Jim's right you know, I'm better at keeping house than thinking about things. My mum was the same, she took care of us and Dad dealt with everything else.'

'And did your dad give your mum a good hiding too if she didn't tow the line?' Jeannie bit her lip and squeezed her friend's hand. 'Come on. Aren't you eating? There'll be nothing left of you when I come home...if I come home.' She pushed a pack of sandwiches across the table. 'It was a BOGOF and you know my eyes are bigger than my belly.'

Margo smiled gratefully. 'Today's turning into a good day. An unexpected lunch and look what I found on the bus, so now I can get chips for tea.' As she pulled the paper out of her bag something fell on the floor.

'Margo! Have you been gambling?' Jeannie laughed as she retrieved the fallen scratch card.

'No! I...it must have been in the paper.'

'This could be your ticket to freedom. Imagine!'

'I should be so lucky. I couldn't even win an argument.' Margo put the card and newspaper back in her bag, 'Come on, let's get back before Maura starts moaning.'

+   +

Jim kissed the wad of money. You beauty! He'd known *FarFlungPlaces* was a dead cert. It must have been from listening to Margo whingeing on about that silly bitch mate of hers going off round the world.

He'd never liked that Jeannie. Stuck up cow. Even at school she'd thought she was better than him. She'd done her best to stop Margo getting with him too but he knew how to turn on the charm when he wanted to. What Miss Jeannie needed was a good man to put her in her place and boy he wished it had been him, but then, she was a feisty one. She'd be hard to handle whereas Margo was a doddle. He just wished he could be a fly on the wall when she was stuck in the arse end of nowhere surrounded by foreigners.

Chuckling to himself at the thought, he shoved his money carefully in his pocket and set off back to the Crown. Wait till he told the lads about his win, that would show them. Load of bloody doubting Thomases. He wasn't going to let on how much he'd won mind but he'd certainly stand them all a drink or three.

+   +

Margo put her tea on the table and sat, enjoying the luxury of the one remaining unbroken chair. She really hoped Jim would drink just enough to make him fall asleep in front of the TV tonight. She didn't think she could cope with his games after today. She wished she had Jeannie's nerve; she'd never even heard of some of the places she was going to visit. It cost nothing to dream though.

She reached into her bag for the travel itinerary that Jeannie had proudly given her and her fingers found the scratch card. Hidden Treasures it said enticingly in gold writing. £300,000 top prize. Wouldn't that be lovely? On impulse, she took a coin from her purse and started to scratch, picking up speed as the silver shark disappeared. Moving down to scratch at the corresponding shark symbol she thought how wonderful it would be if you could eliminate all predators by simply rubbing them out.

A number three appeared, quickly followed by a zero. She felt her heart flutter. Had she really won thirty pounds? No...wait...three hundred...oh my God...the zero's kept appearing as if by magic.

A sudden noise outside made her jump and she froze, listening intently. Please God don't let him come home yet. She pushed the scratch card into her bag and stood, poised to look busy, but everything was quiet again. Breathing out she grabbed her bag. What was she going to do? This didn't happen to people like her. Stumbling through a daze of confusion into the hall she grabbed her coat. Jeannie would check it for her. She would know what to do.

+ +

Jim was cold and there was something hard under his head. Rolling to one side he stared at the lavender bush. What the hell! He sat up carefully. He could vaguely remember banging on the front door but the bitch wouldn't let him in. He anxiously felt in his pocket and pulled out some notes. Thank God. He could have been robbed, lying out here all night. Putting his hand underneath him he winced as something sharp dug into his palm. His key. Vindictive cow must have thrown it out of the window. She wasn't half going to get it.

'Margo!' he bellowed, stumbling into the hall. 'Get here now.'

She must be hiding. Or maybe she'd gone to work early, stepping over him as he lay in the dirt. He wouldn't put it past her. Well, she would keep. His mouth was like the bottom of a birdcage, he needed a drink.

+ +

Drops of rain began to hit the windows as the bus pulled into the airport. Margo watched the crowds of people hurrying into the shelter of the Departures Hall, smiling, and laughing despite the weather, looking forward to sun, sea, and new adventures. She wondered if any of them were secretly waiting for the bubble to burst, expecting to wake up and find it was all a dream. Like she was. She checked her watch, stretching her legs as they threatened a nervous quiver. Their flight left in four hours.

Was it really only six weeks since she'd found the scratch card? It still felt surreal. A delighted Jeannie had taken her in that night and calmed her down. The next day she'd helped her to claim the money and start setting herself up for a brand new life. She'd also dealt with a furious Jim when he came hammering on her door the next evening, shouting that he knew Margo was there because no one else would bloody have her. While Margo hid, Jeannie had given him short shrift, telling him she wasn't surprised Margo had finally seen sense and that he'd better hope she hadn't done anything stupid, because the whole town knew how he treated her and he'd be the prime suspect. He had finally slunk off muttering vague threats and they hadn't seen or heard from him since.

'I can't believe this is happening, Jeannie. I keep expecting Jim to turn up and make me go home.'

'No way! He's too much of a coward to make a show in public. And anyway, I bet he hasn't been further than the bookies and the Crown in years. He'd never find his way here.'

'You're right, I know you are. I just can't believe I've managed to get away. I feel so very lucky.'

'Someone was definitely looking out for you that day.' Jeannie started down the steps, turning excitedly to the hesitant Margo, 'Come on then. Our new lives are waiting.'

Throwing back her shoulders, Margo took a deep breath, then, linking arms with Jeannie she allowed herself to be pulled into the cheerful crowd.

Rosemary Marks

November 30

Every Disturbed Minute

The voice on the phone was cold, remote. Letty listened quietly as he went over everything again. She knew better than to interrupt. It would be pointless anyway, he wouldn't hear her. Tears fell as she listened to him ripping himself apart again. Not in a rage, but in that flat dispassionate voice that she knew only too well. He hadn't always been this way. But these days he wasn't any other way. He was lost, somewhere between recrimination and confession.

"It's time you got some sleep," she said, when he paused for a moment. "Go to bed now, and try to sleep tonight. Goodnight." He grunted, but he ended the call.

Slowly, Letty returned to her bed. The warm spot she had made earlier was gone, and the hot-water bottle was tepid. 'Typical,' she thought, 'and just when I really wanted an early night.' She looked over at the clock glowing on the chest of drawers. 2.42 am. She'd been listening to him talk round in circles for over an hour. And now she couldn't relax, keeping an ear out in case the phone rang again. Fearing it would. But it didn't, and she eventually slept.

Bright sunlight woke her, and she knew she was going to be late for work. Not that that was important. She rang Nigel's number, but as usual his phone was switched off, so she rang her secretary and told him she would be working from home that day. Then she rang the hospital.

Nigel was still quiet, they said. She didn't tell them he'd called her in the small hours. Maybe she should have, but there again, it wasn't that unusual for him to phone, and they knew that. "You shouldn't worry about him. We're looking after him. Leave it to us." The brisk voice of Nurse Margery.

"But he's in such torment. And please, don't tell me it's not real, it is to him. He's my little brother, and I care!" She almost shouted the last three words.

The truth was, she was tired. Midnight calls from Nigel, or the police when he went missing: trekking over to the hospital with his clean washing, taking him chocolate, paper and paints: the sadness of handing these over to strangers because Nigel wouldn't come out of his room to see her. It all added up, and she wasn't in the best of health herself. She was just too tired to have a life. She put it all into fighting for Nigel, so that he could have a life again. Hopefully.

"He's my baby brother," she whispered to the wall. And tears fell silently. Again.

EE Blythe

If you have enjoyed
A Story for Every Day of Autumn,
look out for our next anthology,
A Story for Every Day of Winter.

www.rugbycafewriters.com

And don't miss

Press Pause: Relax with a poem

A collection of thought-provoking poems
also from the Cafe Writers of Rugby.

Available from Amazon

www.rugbycafewriters.com

About the authors

David G Bailey from East Anglia has also lived in Europe, the Caribbean, North and South America, with a base in Rugby for over 40 years. His story (*Salad Dodger*) in this volume is an edited extract from a memoir he aims to publish in 2024, to follow three novels: *Seventeen*, an adventure fantasy story aimed at and beyond young adults; *Them Roper Girls*, tracing the turbulent lives of four sisters from their 1950s childhood; and in 2023 *Them Feltwell Boys*, the (mis)adventures man and boy of one of them Ropers' husbands. To read more of and about David's work, including a quarterly newsletter and new content daily comprising extracts from diaries and other writings, visit his website www.davidgbailey.com.

Pam Barton began writing again recently after many years. In the past, she has had a radio programme for children, been a D.J. and put through the landing on the moon for the Australian Radio in the Indian Ocean. On returning to England, she was a busy parent with John, and became a skin care consultant up to District Manager. After moving again, she went to Luton University for a marketing course. She retired to Rugby with John. Now she is enjoying writing again, painting is also a great pleasure although, as with the writing, hard work is needed.

EE Blythe is compelled to write. And that's all that needs to be said.

David J Boulton took up writing well into retirement from a career in the NHS, so far publishing three historical detective novels. Set in the Peak District, their protagonist has a Quaker background and the books comprise a trilogy. A fourth novel, set in the Second World War, is complete and he has embarked on a sequel. Alongside General Practice, he and his wife have run a small farm in Northamptonshire for the last thirty years. Of their two grown-up children, one lives in the Peak District with her family, their son completing a five-generation connection for the author with the area. The Writing Fiction class at the

Percival Guildhouse tutored by Gill Vickery has provided the author with encouragement and inspiration, not to mention improving his grammar.

***

Patrick Garrett was born in a farm cottage in Perthshire, Scotland before the NHS came to be and spent the first nine years of his life on farms in Perthshire, Peeblesshire, Wigtownshire and Lanarkshire before moving to England, then two more farms in Princethorpe and Dunchurch. His father then moved to Rugby.

As Patrick is blessed with mild dyslexia, his academic career was not stellar but once he learned to read, the world became his oyster. His careers ranged from apprentice, shop assistant, removals, HGV one driver and positions in the warehouse industry. He learned to fly gliders then qualified as a CAA Microlight aircraft pilot having his flying stories published in a flying magazine. After he retired, he decided to take up local history research and write about Rugby's history. He then found Rugby Cafe Writers and says the future is yet to be written.

***

Wendy Goulstone began writing plays from the age of four when given a model theatre, then for performing in story-time in primary school, where she was encouraged by a wonderful headmaster who introduced her to poetry. When eleven years old, she wrote a dramatised version of Little Women and a novel about a group of theatre-mad children. She directed plays at teacher training college, lived in Australia and New Zealand for four years, and on return to the UK, studied for a BA with the Open University and became a member of Rugby Theatre and several writing groups. She continues to write short plays and organises Open Mics for poets and singers. Several of her poems have been published in literary magazines and anthologies and one won *The Oldie* poetry competition!

***

Simon Grenville is a former management trainee with the Orbit Housing Association concerned with rehousing the homeless in Milton Keynes and Central London. He is one the founding members of the

Islington Community Housing Co-operative, North London, the East-West Theatre Company (Geoffrey Ost Memorial Award, University of Sheffield 1980) and the Alexandra Kollantai Film Corporation (2017). Currently trending on the Really TV Channel as Detective Inspector Paul Jones in *Nurses Who Kill*, Episode 1, Director Chris Jury. Training: Rose Bruford College.

Christine Hancock, originally from Essex, lived in Rugby for over forty years. A passion for Family History led to an interest in local history, especially that of the town of Rugby. In 2013 she joined a class at the Percival Guildhouse with the aim of writing up her family history research. The class was Writing Fiction and soon she found herself deep in Anglo-Saxon England. Based on the early life of Byrhtnoth, Ealdorman of Essex, who died in 991AD at the Battle of Maldon, the novel grew into a series. She self-published four volumes followed by the first volume of a new series, *The Wulfstan Mysteries*.

Sadly Christine passed away in December 2021. We remember her with great fondness.

Sally Harper is a member of Rugby Cafe Writers.

Kate A Harris and her three siblings lived on their farm near Market Harborough. She left home at 16 to pursue her career with children. After training in the Morley Manor, Dr. Barnardo's Home, in Derbyshire from 1966 to 1968, she qualified as a Nursery Nurse. Kate met and married her Royal Naval husband in Southsea when working in a children's home. As a naval wife, she was in Malta for two years with her two sons when they were shutting the naval base. They have two sons and two grandchildren. She worked on the local newspaper and discovered a love of writing at 50! Now she is writing her story mainly featuring Barnardo's. It's a major challenge with intense and fascinating research. She's had an incredible response from diverse and fascinating resources. Kate is interested in hearing from people who worked in Barnardo's, mainly in the 1960s.

Cathy Hemsley has been writing short stories and full-length novels for over twelve years: inspired by her family history and by her child's idea for a fantasy novel. Two of her stories have been published in *The People's Friend* and she has completed a fantasy duology, *The Gifts* and *The City*, as well as a book of short stories, *Parable Lives*, all available on Amazon. She is now retired from paid work, working on another two novels, supporting a local church, growing organic vegetables, and is also helping local people as the Rugby advocate for the Acts435 charity.

Jim Hicks was born and raised in Rugby. After leaving school, he studied computing at Imperial College, London and the University of Cambridge. He worked in the Computing Services department of the University of Warwick for nearly twenty-six years before being made redundant in 2011.

His mother is a little surprised that he joined a writers' group. He thought someone might want some help with the technical side of using a computer to prepare documents, and has remained ever since.

Geoff Hill is a Zimbabwean writer and journalist living in Johannesburg. He is chief Africa Correspondent for *The Washington Times* (DC) and maintains a second home in Rugby. In 2000, Geoff became the first non-American to receive a John Steinbeck award for his writing. He has authored two books on Zimbabwe and writes for The Spectator.

John Howes was born and raised in Rugby. He was a journalist on local newspapers for 25 years before retraining as a teacher. He has self-published two books – *We Believe*, a collection of his writings on spirituality, and a guide on how to teach poetry. He plays the piano and writes music for schools and choirs. John is working on a memoir and dabbles in poetry. He runs a book group and is a member of St Andrew's Community Choir. He presents a Youtube Channel on the music of Elton John.

Ruth Hughes was born in Sutton Coldfield but has lived in Rugby for 50 years. She says, "I think I have a book in me but so far I just enjoy writing poems and recollections of my life." Ruth belongs to Murder 57, which enacts murder mysteries around the country, and to Rugby Operatic Society.

Rosemary Marks has lived in Rugby all her life and has three children and three grandchildren. She has always been an avid reader and was lucky enough to work at Rugby Library for 23 years, a Bibliophile's dream. She is now retired and enjoys travelling with her husband, writing, painting, researching her family history and spending time with friends and family.

Peter Maudsley was a member of Rugby Cafe Writers for several years and a good friend to many of us. *Sadly, Peter passed away at the beginning of 2023. He is much missed.*

Madalyn Morgan was brought up in a pub in Lutterworth, where she has returned after living in London for thirty-six years. She had a hairdressing salon in Rugby before going to Drama College. Madalyn was an actress for thirty years, performing on television, in the West End and in Repertory Theatre. She has been a radio journalist and is now presenting classic rock on radio. She has written articles for music magazines, women's magazines and newspapers. She now writes poems, short stories and novels. She has written ten novels – a wartime saga and a post war series. She is currently writing her memoir and a novel for Christmas 2023.

Fran Neatherway grew up in a small village in the middle of Sussex. She studied History at the University of York and put her degree to good use by working in IT. Reading is an obsession – she reads six or seven books a week. Her favourites are crime, fantasy and science fiction. Fran has been writing for thirty-odd years, short stories at first. She has attended several writing classes and has a certificate in Creative Writing from Warwick University. She has completed three children's novels, as yet unpublished, and is working on the first draft of an adult novel. Fran has red hair and lives in Rugby with her husband and no cats.

Simon Parker grew up and lived on The Wirral until 1985. He arrived in Rugby in 2003 via Coventry, Bristol and Seattle. He's an aerospace engineer by training, with a love of the open road whether by bicycle, motorcycle or car. His travels galvanise his writing and he writes fiction for pleasure. He lives with his wife, two teenage children and a small collection of interesting vehicles: 'on the button' and ready for their next adventure!

Steve Redshaw was born and raised in Sussex. Over the past forty years he has taught young children in the South of England and East Anglia. He has now retired and is living aboard his narrowboat, Miss Amelia, on the Oxford Canal near Rugby. His passion is music, singing and playing guitar, and various other plucked instruments, in pubs, folk clubs and sessions around the area. He also is a dance caller for Barn Dances and Ceilidhs. His creative output is perhaps best described as emergent and sporadic, but when time allows, he enjoys composing songs and writing short stories.

Chris Rowe. Just before covid, Chris tried to write poetry: lockdown gave the time to attempt different poetic forms, some of which appeared in *Press Pause*. From childhood, Chris has been interested in reading prose: such as Richmal Crompton (*Just William*), Alison Utley (*Sam Pig*), Henry Fielding, Mark Twain, Jane Austen, and Terry Pratchett.

Shakespeare has always been a favourite and long ago the ambition was achieved of seeing a performance of every play: *Antony and Cleopatra* being the hardest to track down (all those scene changes deter production.). Favourite performers of the Bard are Oddsocks.

Linda Slate has lived in Rugby for 11 years. She has four children, 15 grandchildren and three great-grandchildren. She has worked as a teacher and a police officer, both jobs have given her inspiration for her writing. Along with swimming, writing has been a lifelong passion. She has not yet had a novel published, but hopes to have one ready to submit by the end of 2023.

Christopher Trezise was born and raised in Rugby and pursued a professional acting career on theatre stages culminating in work for Disneyland Paris. Christopher has held many jobs from kitchen assistant through to risk management consultant but he has always had a passion for writing. He runs several table-top roleplaying groups which he writes scenarios for and has self-published a fantasy book based upon one of those games.

Lindsay Woodward has had a lifelong passion for writing, starting off as a child when she used to write stories about the Fraggles of *Fraggle Rock*. Knowing there was nothing else she'd rather study, she did her degree in writing and has now turned her favourite hobby into a career. She writes from her home in Rugby, where she lives with her husband and cat. When she's not writing, Lindsay runs a Marketing Agency, where she spends most of her time copywriting, so words really are her life. Her debut novel, *Bird*, was published in April 2016, and Lindsay's 9th novel is due to be released in 2023.

Fiona White was brought up in St Andrew's where summer jobs in local hotels gave her early writing material. Whilst enjoying writing as a teenager – especially poetry – she abandoned this creative side of herself for more than 25 years, building a successful career in business where she worked in both finance and sales.

Her re-engagement with writing has its roots in memoir but she is also interested in writing from a more historical perspective, encompassing her love for history and old ruins. Having moved around the UK in her work, Fiona is now settled in Rugby with her husband and dog. She does some non-executive director work and freelance coaching. She enjoys golf, swimming and walking with friends.

Chris Wright says the following:
My earliest memory is of my mother using flashcards
to teach me to read while still in my playpen
we lived in a flat at West Heath,
a Vimto only area of Birmingham,
so my poetry is restricted
to about fifty different words
usually including "hippopotamus"

Printed in Great Britain
by Amazon

27072841R00131